MW01048016

Holding On

Lana Voynich

This is a work of fiction. Names, characters, businesses, places, events and incidents are either the products of the author's imagination or used in a fictitious manner. Any resemblance to reality is purely coincidental.

Cover design by Lori Gnahn.
Editing by Red Adept Editing.

ISBN:1540780627
ISBN-13: 978-1540780621

Dedication

Another one for my parents. I love and miss you both.

Acknowledgments

Without Alyssa, Neila, Kristina, and Lynn this book wouldn't be nearly what it is today. Thank you for your help and insights. You guys are the best!

Chapter 1

HEARING A KEY in the lock of the apartment door, Kylie Killian grimaced and slid the Christmas card from her ex-boyfriend, Tom Mallock, into her art textbook. She ran her hands over her face and smoothed her hair, hoping to hide the fact that she'd been sitting there daydreaming about her past with Tom, when Lance Mallock walked into their apartment.

"Hey. Where have you been?" she asked from the worn couch that had come with the furnished apartment the school had found for her in Traverse City, Michigan.

He held up a plastic shopping bag. "I needed a few things for supper."

"I could have stopped at the store on my way home if you'd told me."

He set the bag on the harvest-gold kitchen counter and crossed to the couch in three strides. "I wanted some air."

When he bent to kiss her, she reached up to twine her fingers behind his neck and pull him closer. She loved having him with her, loved having someone to talk to about her daily life, and loved having someone who cared about her. *I love having someone to take my mind off…* Instead of finishing her thought about Tom and their son, she shifted closer to Lance and caressed the side of his throat.

After a few moments, Lance shifted away and ran his hand through his short brown hair. "I need to get supper started."

"Why? I thought things were already cooking." Kylie caught his wrist and tugged, hoping he would join her on the couch and wipe all thoughts of his brother from her mind.

He shook his head and backed away. "I know how cranky you get when you're hungry. I have everything ready to go except the salad."

She frowned but stood. "What are we having, and what should I do to help?"

"You can set the table while I get the chicken out of the

oven."

Kylie began gathering the dishes and silverware. "How was your day?"

"Okay. My mom called."

Her eyebrows arched, but she carefully smoothed her expression before facing him. "What's new with her?"

He set the roasted chicken on a cutting board and selected a knife from the drawer. "She wanted to know if I was coming home to Minnesota for Christmas."

She leaned against the counter and crossed her arms. "Are you?"

They hadn't discussed Christmas even though it was less than two weeks away. She was perfectly content to stay right there with Lance. It would be the first Christmas in eleven years that she hadn't been alone. Except maybe he would go back to Chinkapin—the tiny town where they had grown up in northeastern Minnesota, and she would be alone in Michigan. Maybe he would choose his lying, child-stealing parents over her.

His brow wrinkled as he shifted his gaze away. "I haven't decided."

She pressed her lips together and nodded. "I see." All her thoughts and excitement about spending the holidays with him in their crappy little apartment crumbled as she straightened and moved away from the counter. Crossing to the living room window, Kylie stared out at the snowflakes floating past the lights in the parking lot.

"What do you want to do for Christmas?"

"I hadn't given it much thought." She didn't want to tell him she'd been obsessively fantasizing about spending it with him since Thanksgiving. She'd pictured the two of them cuddling under a blanket on the ratty couch with twinkling lights on a tree, while they watched *The Yule Log*. After making love, they would fall asleep on the couch and wake in the morning when the sun shone through their tiny second-story window.

"Well, come sit down. We'll talk about it while we eat."

Forcing a smile, she returned to the table. Even with her churning stomach, she would force herself to eat. He'd cooked chicken because it was her favorite. "If you want to go to your parents', it's fine. I understand."

"You're invited too. You know that, right?"

She met his gaze. "Why would they invite me? Why would they think I'd have anything to do with them after what they did to Tom and I?"

"They invited you because I love you. I assume they want to make amends."

"Make amends? How does that happen?"

"I don't know, Kylie, but you were invited." He reached across the tiny table to take her hand in his. "I know they hurt you, and I know you're still angry, but they're my family."

"I'm perfectly well aware that they're your family, but they sold my son. They paid someone at Middleton School for Girls to tell me Erick died so someone could adopt him." She took a deep breath. "So I couldn't raise him. So their precious son's name wasn't sullied by a girl from the wrong side of town."

"You don't know that."

She freed her hand to rake her unruly red hair back then twisted it into a knot. "Fine. I don't know what they did with Erick, but we both know they were in cahoots with Middleton. It's been four months since we found out Erick is alive, and I still don't know where he is." *Or if I even want to meet him.*

Lance nodded. "Fair enough."

"Have you heard anything from Tom lately?" She fought the urge to clamp a hand over her mouth and tell him to forget she asked, but she knew that would draw more suspicion than the question.

"No, why?"

She thought of the card in her book. It was more than just a standard Christmas card that came twenty to a box. It was a single one Tom had selected from a display because it meant something. Or maybe he'd hoped it would mean something to her. He'd sent it to her at the school instead of there at the apartment. "I was curious how he's doing after his accident. Is his leg better?" What she really wanted to know was whether or not he was going to Chinkapin for Christmas.

"Mom said that she's been talking to Eva. Tom won't talk to her or Dad."

Kylie let out her breath. If Tom wasn't talking to his parents, then he wouldn't be in Chinkapin for Christmas.

"He's still with Eva in Montana?"

"Yeah." Lance took another bite of chicken.

"Good. She seemed like she really cares about him." When Kylie had returned to Chinkapin the previous summer, she'd been nervous about seeing Tom but hopeful. It hadn't gone well at all, and he'd refused to talk to her. Knowing he was happy with Eva should have made Kylie happier than it did.

Lance and Kylie ate in silence. After her plate was empty, she stood.

"Hang on. You never told me what you want to do. Or how you normally spend Christmas."

She scraped her teeth over her bottom lip. "I normally spend Christmas alone, drawing." She forced a grin. "Surprising, huh?"

Lance scratched the back of his neck. "Why?"

She laughed, hoping to hide how much it hurt to admit the truth. "What else would I do? My parents don't invite me to join them."

"What about Mira and Keefe?"

Mira had been Kylie's best friend since elementary school. Just recently, Mira had reconnected with her high school boyfriend, Kylie's cousin, Bryon O'Keefe. "What about them? They invited me, but they have their own things going on. I don't want to intrude."

"It's not intruding if you're invited."

She set her dishes in the sink and turned on the hot water. "Mira goes to her grandparents' place in Chicago, and Keefe goes to his mom's. It's awkward because his parents don't know why my parents and I don't get along. His mom hounds me the whole time about being distant from my mother."

His chair scraped as he pushed back from table, and she tensed as she focused on scrubbing the dishes, afraid if she saw pity in his expression, she would cry. He stopped behind her and wrapped his arms around her in a hug. As he burrowed his face into the side of her neck, she relaxed.

"If you want to stay here, I'll stay with you. No more lonely Christmases for you."

Her hands stilled in the hot water. "What about your family?" She couldn't imagine them not being upset with him. Every encounter she'd had with Lance and Tom's parents had convinced her that they were selfish and used to having everything they wanted when they wanted it.

"What about them? I've spent twenty-six Christmases with them. They'll survive one without me."

She turned in his arms and met his gaze. "Really? You'd do that for me?"

"Of course. Just tell me what you want."

She dried her hands on the dish towel from the counter then leaned against him to wrap her arms around his neck as she considered it. He was selfless enough to give up his traditions for her, and he'd come here with her. He hadn't seen his family since they'd left Montana after Tom's accident. It was only fair that she gave up something for him. She nodded. "My fellowship is done at the end of the week. Let's go to Chinkapin for Christmas."

His face broke into a smile, and he lifted her off her feet and twirled her in a circle. "Really?"

"Sure. We're going back in February for Mira's wedding, anyway. We can go to Chinkapin later this week and stay at my house until after the wedding." She'd considered selling it but hadn't contacted a realtor yet, so at least they had a comfortable place to stay while they were in Minnesota. There was no way she would ever consider staying with Lance's parents. Dinner was already pushing the limits of how much time she wanted to spend with them. She doubted they would say anything that would help her find Erick, but maybe she could convince Lance to ask them what had happened.

His smile grew even wider. "That sounds awesome. Will you come with me to my parents' house on Christmas Eve?"

She grimaced. "Probably, but even if I don't, at least we'll be in the same town."

Chapter 2

TOM MALLOCK LIMPED out of the bedroom he shared with Eva in Missoula. It'd been three months since the car accident, and his doctors had told him his broken leg was healed. He just wished they'd told his leg. It didn't seem to understand everything was better. It still got tired if he stood or walked too long. When he sat too long, it got stiff and painful. He couldn't seem to find a happy medium, and he was tired of being limited in what he could do.

He grumbled under his breath as he lowered himself on the couch and propped his right leg up on the coffee table. Rubbing his thigh, he reached for the glass of Scotch on the side table. Drinking was about the only thing that made his leg feel almost normal. Unfortunately, it wasn't helping any other part of his life.

A spicy floral scent enveloped him, and he knew Eva was standing behind the couch. "Who called?" He'd heard the phone when he got out of the shower and purposely took his time drying off and dressing.

"Your mom."

Tom sighed. "Great. Did you have a nice chat?" Since he'd learned of his parents' part in his son's disappearance, Tom had had nothing to do with them. His lack of communication didn't seem to deter them, though. When his mom had realized he wouldn't answer her calls, she had started calling Eva's phone.

"She wanted to know if we got their card."

Tom shook his head and drained the highball glass. They'd removed his son from his life because they hadn't wanted him and Kylie Killian together forever, and they'd snubbed Eva after the car accident. He couldn't understand why Eva accepted his mother's calls, let alone talked to her. When he'd asked about it, Eva had simply said, "She's your mother. She loves you even if she makes mistakes."

When he didn't say anything, Eva leaned down to hug him from behind the couch. "You know they love you."

"Yeah. Right." He enjoyed her touch for a moment then scooted forward on the couch, pushing off the arm and gritting his teeth until he was upright. He grabbed his empty glass and rounded the end of the sofa, walking into the kitchen area of the duplex Eva had found while he'd been in the hospital. The table wasn't big enough for two people to dine at so it had been relegated to serve as a bar and junk mail collection area. He set the glass down and pushed the Scotch bottle aside. His current mood, since learning of his mother's phone call, warranted something other than Scotch, something as fierce as his mood.

He unscrewed the cap of a tequila bottle and filled his glass. It wasn't his preferred drink for relaxing, but he didn't want to relax. He wanted to forget everything, including his parents and how they conned Middleton School for Girls into adopting out his son and lying to Kylie. He wanted to forget that his investigator hadn't found his son yet, and that the lawyer he'd spoken to had said it was unclear whether a judge would ever give his son to him since the boy had been living with another family for eleven years. He wanted to forget that Kylie—the love of his life—was now living in Michigan with his younger brother and hadn't responded to the Christmas card he'd mailed her. He wanted to forget the accident that left him hobbling like a ninety-year-old drunk. And he really wanted to forget that Eva's touch hadn't turned him on since he'd woken up from the coma after his accident and Kylie had been at his bedside holding his hand.

After he'd settled back on the couch with his drink, Eva sat beside him. "I think you should go home for Christmas and talk to them."

"Why?"

"Because you need to move on. You can't hide in Missoula forever just because Kylie is dating Lance. You have a job and a house in Chinkapin."

"I have a house. I quit the job." When Tom couldn't stand being around his family anymore, he'd resigned from his position running Mallock Enterprises.

Eva patted his leg. "You're letting your anger destroy you.

Go back and prove you're stronger than this."

He took a big swallow of tequila. "I have nothing to prove. They did what they did. They can deal with the consequences."

Eva pursed her lips and looked away. When she turned back, her eyes pleaded with him. "I hate seeing you like this. You won't even talk to Lance."

Tom gazed at the amber liquid in his glass. Even now, he wasn't drunk enough to tell Eva he didn't want to talk to Lance because it reminded him that Kylie hadn't chosen him. After exhaling forcefully, he frowned. "Do you want to go to Chinkapin for Christmas?"

She shook her head. "Not at all. I just want you to be happy."

"And you think seeing my family will make me happy, knowing what they did?"

"I know what your parents did. I don't know what Lance did." She tipped her head to the side and brushed her blond hair out of her face. Then she trailed her hand up the inside of his leg, starting at his knee.

When he stopped her hand and shifted away, she frowned. "Unless you're upset that he's with Kylie."

"Not likely." He could deny it all he wanted, but he couldn't look Eva in the eye. "I'm upset that he thinks I should forgive our parents."

"You know you're allowed to disagree with your family. It doesn't mean you have to disown them."

"Why the big push for me to go for Christmas? You can't really care about my family."

"I told you. I want you to be happy. I thought you and Lance were close."

"Are you going to come with me?" He hoped she would decline. He'd been looking for a way to avoid her for the past two months.

She crossed her legs then uncrossed them. A second later, she stood and went into the kitchen.

He twisted on the couch to watch as she rearranged the booze bottles. "Eva, what's going on?"

She faced him and lifted her shoulders in a shrug. "Some friends invited me to Colorado to go skiing."

He nodded slowly. "And you don't want me to go with."

"It's not that. It's just…" Her shoulders drooped. "What fun would you have sitting around the lodge, waiting for us to come back in?"

"And what fun would you have with me sitting around?" He turned back to the TV. Finally, he would be alone and not have to hide his misery. "So go skiing. It's fine. I can take care of myself."

She sighed. "Lance called too. He's going home for Christmas and really wants to see you."

Tom felt like an owl as his head spun around. "Is Kylie going with him?" The possibility of seeing Kylie was more enticing than hearing what Lance had to say.

"I didn't ask. I just told him I'd talk to you about it."

He growled under his breath. "Why?" His family just didn't get the picture that he didn't want to be in contact with them. If he wanted to visit at Christmas, he certainly knew how to find his way home.

"I'm not leaving you here alone for Christmas."

"I'm a big boy. I can handle it."

She walked over to crouch in front of him. "I'm worried about you. Not physically but mentally. The holidays have the highest suicide rates of the entire year."

He chuckled humorlessly. He had no desire to sip eggnog with his family and listen to his nieces and nephews sing carols. However, there was a pretty good chance that if Lance was going, Kylie would go too. He couldn't imagine Kylie staying in Michigan if Lance was returning to Minnesota. If he went home, he could see her. He could find out if the way she was looking at him when he woke from his coma meant something. They could reminisce and comfort one another.

He covered Eva's hand with his. "If it means that much to you, I'll go, but I'm coming back as soon as I can get a flight after Christmas."

"Thank you." She squeezed his hand gently then kissed his cheek. "You know you've been talking about finding Erick for a while. Maybe you can convince Kylie to help find him. She must know more about him than you do."

"How could she? They told her he was dead and gave him to someone else."

"I don't know, but if she's on your side about finding him,

maybe she'll be able to convince a judge that you two should have joint custody."

He couldn't imagine that Kylie wouldn't want custody of Erick. Even if Kylie wouldn't reconcile with Tom, Erick was a binder between them. If the boy were returned to their lives, Tom and Kylie would always have that bond. They would always have Erick holding them together, forcing them to see one another. Maybe someday, she would realize she was with the wrong brother.

* * *

Tom eased into the bed, hoping not to disturb Eva. He'd stared at the television for two hours after she'd gone to bed in the hope that she would fall asleep before he came to the bedroom. It had been three days since he'd agreed to go home for Christmas. She was leaving for Colorado the next morning, and he was flying to Minnesota.

"Mmm. You're finally here," Eva whispered as she rolled over and pressed against him.

Dammit. "Yeah. I didn't mean to wake you." He tried to shift away, but she draped a leg over his hip and kissed the side of his throat.

"I don't mind."

Her hand caressed his chest, and he froze. He'd been able to head off her advances for months, but tonight she seemed more determined. When her hand slipped under the waistband of his boxers, he grabbed her wrist.

"Not tonight," he said and kissed the top of her head.

Eva jerked free and rolled away to turn on the bedside lamp, then she faced him. "What the hell is going on?"

"I'm just not in the mood." He cursed himself for even coming to bed. He should have stayed on the couch and drank until he passed out.

"You expect me to believe that? You're a freaking horndog. Remember? We used to have sex a couple times a night, but not anymore. Not in months. Not since the accident."

Tom tried to ignore the tremble in her voice and the moisture gathering in her eyes, but he couldn't. "It's not you. It's just…" He stood. "I'll sleep on the couch."

As he walked to the door, a pillow hit his shoulder.

"Dammit, Tom, tell me what the hell is going on. Are you screwing someone else?"

Unable to prevent himself, he chuckled. His brother lived with the only other woman he wanted to be with. "Of course not."

"So you're just not attracted to me anymore?"

He rubbed his forehead and looked away as he lied. "It's not that. I just don't know that I can do it."

As her eyes narrowed into a glare, he moved back to the bed. "Since the accident, I don't know if I can."

Eva peered at him for a few moments. "Seriously?"

He nodded. It wasn't a complete lie. He got aroused when he remembered him and Kylie in the bed of his truck in high school, but when Eva touched him, his body didn't react. "It's not something I really want to talk about, though."

"Don't you want to know?"

There was nothing to know other than he wasn't turned on by the thought of having sex with Eva, but he didn't want to talk about it anymore. Just going along with it would be easier. "As long as you realize my performance has no reflection on you."

"I understand. I just don't understand why you didn't say anything until now."

"It's embarrassing."

"Why?" She pushed him until he was lying flat on his back. "Never mind. Just relax and enjoy."

Tom closed his eyes and pictured long auburn hair surrounding them instead of short blond hair as her mouth moved over his, kissing and tasting him. Her hands skimmed over his shoulders and chest, leaving a trail of fire as his skin warmed. When her mouth followed her hands, his body twitched, and he groaned. "You're the best."

Chapter 3

KYLIE SMILED AS she stepped onto the porch of the house she'd inherited from her grandfather. Even though it was only a few miles from Chinkapin—her least favorite place in the world—she loved it. She'd considered selling it simply because she didn't want to be near the town she'd grown up in, but the memories here were almost too good for her to give up. Grandpa would sit in his recliner with her and read *Pokey Little Puppy* over and over until she fell asleep. Grandma taught her how to make blueberry pie in the kitchen. Maybe Christmas here would be as great as Lance had promised.

She made a note to thank Keefe for clearing the sidewalk and step when he'd plowed the driveway.

Kylie unlocked the door and entered, breathing deeply. No matter how long her grandfather had been gone, the house still hinted at the aroma of his pipe tobacco. Every time she returned after an absence, it seemed as if the house hugged her with its scent.

She switched on the light and kicked her heavy winter boots off as Lance came in with their bags.

"If you want to take these, I'll bring in some wood for a fire," he offered.

"Sure. Just set them there, and I'll take them once I get some lights turned on."

Fifteen minutes later, they were snuggled under a patchwork quilt on the couch, sipping coffee laced with Irish Cream. Lance's arm rested on the back of the couch, and he squeezed her shoulder. "Happy to be back?"

"Happy to be right here with you."

"Good."

She shifted closer, resting her head on his shoulder as the fire crackled and snapped. Staring at the flames, her eyelids drooped. She hadn't slept well in the five days since she'd agreed to come back. Now that they were there, she just wanted to fall asleep on the couch, watching the fire, like she had when she was little and spent the night with her grandparents. With the soothing beat of Lance's heart beneath her ear, Grandma's quilt tucked over her, and Lance's arm around her, she sighed and relaxed completely.

She would go visit her parents sometime in the next few days, but for now, all she had to do was relax and enjoy being with Lance.

* * *

The next morning, Kylie was drinking coffee at the kitchen table when a knock sounded at the door. She grinned when she saw Mira on the porch. "Get in here," she called as she stood to pour a cup of coffee for her best friend since elementary school. "What are you doing here?"

Mira draped her multi-colored cloak over the back of a chair and shook the snowflakes from her brown bobbed hair. "I saw Lance in town, and he said you were probably up by now."

"Yeah. When he gets up, he makes enough noise to wake the dead."

"In other words, he's more of a morning person than you?" Mira settled at the table and sipped her coffee. "Of course, a bat is more of a morning person than you."

Kylie smirked. "Probably, but I'm awake now."

"And you're not happy about it?"

"It is what it is." Kylie sighed. "How are things with you and Keefe?"

"Wonderful." Mira's smile was so genuinely happy that Kylie had to smile back.

"I'm thrilled for both of you. How are the wedding plans coming along?"

"Good, but that's not why I came over here. I came to see what the hell is going on with you. Why are you here?"

Kylie frowned. "Lance wanted to come home for Christmas, and I wanted to spend Christmas with him."

"Here?"

Kylie shrugged. "He wants to see his family. I hear some people actually like their family."

"Yeah." Mira folded her arms on the table and leaned

forward, peering at Kylie. "Are you okay? You look awful."

"Tom sent me a Christmas card."

"Why does that have you looking so miserable? Isn't it normal for a guy to send his brother a card?"

Kylie grimaced and shook her head. "No. He sent it to me. At work. No mention of Lance at all. Nor of Eva."

"Well…" Mira drew the word out then took a drink from her cup. "That's"—she shrugged—"different. What did it say?"

After standing and walking to the counter, Kylie stared out the window over the sink for a few seconds. "Just a standard Christmas card," she said, even though she'd memorized it. "You know, 'I hope you have a wonderful holiday season, and you should know I'm thinking of you.'"

"Do you think he's still interested in you?"

"No idea. I thought he and Eva were living together. Wouldn't that make their relationship fairly serious?"

"He hasn't said anything about her to us."

Kylie looked up from her mug. "He's been talking to you guys?"

"Sure. He's Keefe's best man."

Kylie fought to swallow the coffee in her mouth without choking as she realized she would be walking down the aisle with her ex-boyfriend.

"I figured you knew."

She rotated her cup then traced the rim with her middle finger. "I didn't give it much thought."

"I suppose you've had a few other things on your mind—Erick, Lance, your job in Michigan."

"But still, I should pay more attention. I feel like a crappy friend."

"It's okay. Really." Mira patted Kylie's hand. "I promise I'm not going to stop being your friend just because you didn't realize Tom was going to be the best man."

Kylie smiled gratefully. "Tom hasn't talked to Lance since we went back to Michigan."

"Really? I thought they were close. At least they used to be."

"Yeah. They were." Kylie frowned. "I don't know what's going on. Tom was still in the coma when I went out there to be with Lance. When I touched his hand and talked to him, he woke up, and he looked at me like he used to when we were in high school."

Mira propped her chin on her fist, eyes wide. "Like he used to?"

"Yeah. Like he did when he'd wake up after we…" She cleared her throat, thinking better of discussing the aftermath of teenage sex with Tom. "Back when we were dating. Then when Lance put his arm around me, Tom's face changed."

"Changed how?"

"Like he switched something off. I don't know. Maybe it was just the stress of everything. Maybe I imagined it." She knew she hadn't imagined it. Even Lance had noticed Tom's odd behavior.

"Maybe you imagined that your ex-boyfriend still has the hots for you?" Mira's voice showed her disbelief. "What makes you think that he's still interested? He certainly never gave me any clue that he even knew who you were, and I worked with him for years."

"I don't know. It was definitely weird, but when Eva showed up, they were all over each other." She frowned at the gnawing feeling in her stomach.

"Kylie, do you still have feelings for Tom?"

"He's Erick's father. He was my first. Of course I have feelings for him, but I'm not doing anything about them."

"What kind of feelings?"

"I don't know. Curiosity, regret, nostalgia, fond memories. What am I supposed to feel for him?" Even though Mira was her best friend, Kylie couldn't admit to her that she still thought about Tom's kisses or that she still wondered what it would be like if he'd been the Mallock interested in her last summer instead of Lance. She couldn't admit that she still wished Tom had been part of her life for the past eleven years.

"I have no idea. I was just wondering. Does Lance know that you still care about him? That you're uncomfortable around him?"

Kylie shook her head. "Of course not. They're brothers, and they haven't talked in a while. I don't want to do anything to ruin their relationship."

"What about your relationship with Lance?"

Kylie wrapped her arms around herself and ignored Mira's quirked eyebrow. She wasn't hiding anything now. She really didn't know whether she would sacrifice her relationship with Lance for the chance to be with Tom again.

* * *

The next evening, Kylie sat on the couch, staring at the fire, trying to recapture the feeling of contentment she'd had the night they arrived in Chinkapin. She sipped a beer and told herself everything would be fine. It was only four days until Christmas, and she wasn't going to have to see Tom. She could focus on Lance and surviving dinner with his parents. She didn't have to worry about who she would choose if she had a chance to be with Tom again.

She'd cleared her mind enough to relax when she saw the reflection of headlights on the window. Expecting Lance to arrive with some groceries, she went to open the door.

"You're home." She stepped forward to hug Lance then froze. "Tom! What are you doing here?"

"I was wondering if I could stay here a few days."

Her initial reaction was to scream "No!" as loudly as possible, but Lance missed Tom. He never complained or said anything about it, but she knew Tom's absence bothered him. She sighed. "How long?"

"I'm going back to Missoula the day after Christmas."

She knew if she was going to be with Lance, she would have to be around Tom. "Sure. Does Lance know you're back?"

"No. I was going to surprise you guys. Did it work?"

"Yeah. Definitely stunned."

He leaned forward and kissed her cheek. "Thanks for letting me stay. I had no idea The Duck Inn filled up. Ever."

Kylie's breath caught in her throat, and she backed away. A kiss on the cheek from her boyfriend's brother shouldn't cause her heart to bounce in her chest and make it hard to breathe. She forced a laugh. "You seem to forget the hundreds of hotel rooms twenty miles away in Duluth."

His left eyebrow peaked, and he cocked his head. "Do you want me to stay in Duluth? I get it if you don't want me around. I just figured I'd ask. I thought it'd be easier to catch up with Lance if I stayed here."

Already feeling guilty, Kylie shook her head. "No, of course not. You're welcome to stay here. There's a spare room."

Tom peered at her for a second and opened his mouth. Instead of speaking, though, he clamped his mouth shut and looked around. "Where is my brother?"

"He ran to the grocery store." She turned to check the clock. "He should be back any time. I actually thought it was him arriving."

"Nope. Just me."

She leaned forward and looked at the driveway. "How did you get here from the airport?"

"I caught a ride with Vern Tallbaum."

Kylie's breath caught in her throat, and her mouth went dry. After swallowing multiple times, she was able to speak as she turned and led him into the kitchen. "I didn't know you were friends with him."

"I saw him at the airport. I was going to get a taxi, but he offered me a ride."

Kylie wiped her sweaty palms on her jeans and yanked open the fridge to grab two bottles of beer. After opening the first, she offered it to Tom.

He thanked her and reached for the bottle. As his fingers brushed hers, she jerked away.

Tom smiled and backed up. "You okay?"

"Fine." Touching him wasn't something she wanted, yet she'd felt a magnetic pull when their fingers touched. Not only did her mouth go dry, but she wanted to move closer and let him wrap his hand around hers and pull her into an embrace.

She heard boots stomping on the porch and sighed in relief. "Lance must be home." She opened the door and took grocery bags from Lance before moving to the side so he could see his brother.

"Tom! What are you doing here?" Lance stepped forward and wrapped his arms around Tom in a hug.

"I came home for Christmas. Kylie said I could stay here with you guys."

Lance narrowed his eyes. "Really?"

"He just showed up on the porch a few minutes ago and asked me. I'm as shocked as you are." She certainly didn't want

Lance to think that she and Tom had been in contact or that the two of them were planning anything together. "He hasn't even been here long enough to put his bag in the spare room."

"I'll get it," Lance offered and grabbed the suitcase from beside the door. "The spare room?"

"Yes." Kylie turned to the counter with the bags of groceries. She needed to focus on something other than how good Tom had smelled when he kissed her cheek or how gently his fingers had brushed against hers.

"Where's Eva?" Lance asked when he returned to the room.

Kylie sighed in relief that Lance was back and opened a beer for him. When she stood next to him, Lance draped an arm around her shoulders. Unable to meet Tom's gaze, she peeled the edge of the label from her bottle.

"She's skiing in Colorado."

"Oh," Lance said. "Why?"

"Why not? She can ski." Tom rubbed at his thigh then gestured at the kitchen table. "Do you mind if we sit?"

Blinking at her rudeness, Kylie nodded. "Of course not. Sorry. Come into the living room where the furniture is more comfortable. I lit a fire. I love having a fire here."

Tom followed her. "You've always liked fire."

Kylie froze in front of the fireplace, her back to the guys and her face burning. The blush wasn't from the heat of the burning logs, but from the memory of making love with Tom next to a campfire in the woods.

Lance touched her arm. "Kylie…"

She turned toward him. "Hmm?"

"You okay?"

"I'm fine. I was just thinking. Sorry."

Tom hobbled around the room. "This is different than I remember."

Kylie watched him, surprised at his limp. When she'd left Montana with Lance, Tom's prognosis had sounded good. Apparently, the fracture in his leg wasn't healing as well as it should. When she wondered whether or not there were other—more private—lasting injuries from his accident, she forced her mind to focus on Lance's hand on hers. She pressed against his side and kissed his cheek.

"You've been here before?" Lance asked.

Kylie rubbed her forehead and swallowed, irritated Tom was sharing their past with Lance. She'd never gone into detail with Lance about her past before she started dating him last summer. He knew she'd dated Tom and gotten pregnant. "We went swimming once while Grandpa and Grandma were out of town."

Lance raised an eyebrow, clenched his jaw, and nodded. Then he focused on Tom. "Kylie's made lots of changes to the place. It's amazing. Lots has changed."

Kylie took Lance's hand and tugged him to the couch, where they sat side by side.

Tom lowered himself into the recliner beside the fireplace. "It's a great place. I'm glad you didn't sell it."

"Not yet. I'm still thinking about it, though. It's just hard to let it go because of all the memories." She kept her gaze on her bottle as the room fell into silence. She hoped Tom didn't bring up any more of their old memories. She didn't want to be reminded of how easy it had been for her and Tom to end up naked when they were together.

"Have you talked to Mom or Dad?" Lance asked after a few minutes.

"No. I figured I'd just show up and catch them off guard."

Kylie finished her beer and cuddled against Lance, hoping her sense of calm would return as the brothers talked. Their voices faded into the background as she remembered the time she'd brought Tom here. They'd sat in the same recliner he was sitting in now. It had been the first time their kissing had gone beyond kissing, and she'd been about to take him up to the attic when the front door had opened. She'd rushed him out the back door onto the deck and remained inside to visit with her grandparents. Suddenly feeling too warm to snuggle, she moved away from Lance and glanced at him.

"More beer?" he asked.

"No, thanks."

"You seem a million miles away."

Kylie glanced at Tom, who winked. Kylie's face burned again, and she stood. "I think I'm just going to go to bed and let you guys catch up. Holidays are always weird for me."

Lance rose to kiss her, and though she wanted to ignore

Tom, she could feel his gaze. Part of her considered being a lot more affectionate with Lance just because Tom was watching, but everything about his presence made her uncomfortable.

When she stepped away from Lance, she forced a smile at Tom, who stared at her with a slight frown. "There are clean towels in the bathroom next to your room and extra blankets in the closet."

"Thanks." He rose from the chair and shuffled to her then pulled her into a one-armed hug. He hugged Lance with the other arm. "You guys are great. Thanks for letting me stay."

"Of course," Lance replied.

Kylie forced another smile and backed away, regretting her agreement to this. There was no way the next six days wouldn't be uncomfortable, and no way those days could go fast enough.

Chapter 4

ONCE THE GUYS were settled back in the living room with more beer, Lance turned to Tom and narrowed his eyes. "You've been here before?"

"Yeah, when we were dating, we came here once. We fooled around a little." Tom took a drink of his beer and grimaced. "Do you have anything else to drink?"

"No. We're not into hard liquor. All we have is beer."

"Figures." Tom laughed. "Are you still upset that Kylie and I have a past?"

Lance sighed. "I'm working on it. It was a lot easier before I knew you fooled around with her here."

"What's the big deal? You know that we have a kid together. It's pretty clear that we've done more than fool around."

"Yeah. I just don't want to spend all my time in this house, wondering where you and my girlfriend have been naked together."

"Nowhere. We weren't naked. We just—"

Lance waved his hand. "I don't want details. I don't want to know anything about it."

Tom shook his head. "You're going to have to get over it. Everyone has a past."

"I know. Like I said, I'm working on it." He set his beer bottle on the end table, leaned back, and crossed his ankles on the coffee table. "How are things with you and Eva?"

Tom considered lying and saying everything was great. He knew it would ease some of Lance's worries about his presence, but he was tired of lying to protect people's feelings. "Not the best."

"Why? What happened? You guys seemed fine when we left Montana."

"We were never supposed to be anything serious. I'm not sure she remembers that."

"She's been with you for months. It sure seemed serious.

You seemed determined to stay with her in Montana."

"I was determined to stay away from our parents." Tom stared at the fire for a few minutes. Discussing his love life with Lance seemed inappropriate. How could he talk about Eva when all he wanted was to be with Kylie?

Lance leaned forward to pat Tom's knee. "You're fine, right? Is there something you didn't tell me?"

"No. The doctors say my leg is healed. I'm done with my physical therapy. It should get better as my muscles get stronger." *I didn't tell you that I still dream about Kylie. Or that when I woke up in the hospital, it felt like when I woke up after having sex with her—a little confused and unwilling to return to reality.*

Lance relaxed back into the couch. "You'll be back to your old self in no time."

Tom turned his attention back to the fire. "Yeah. Maybe." He'd forgotten about the one time he and Kylie had been there until he stepped into the living room. She hadn't reacted the way he'd hoped when he commented on the fire, but the redness in her cheeks—which also happened when they were having sex—made it clear she knew exactly what he was referring to. Right now, though, he just wanted to sit in the chair and remember the experience. He wanted to remember what it had been like to be seventeen and so in love that he didn't care about anything other than his fifteen-year-old girlfriend. He'd been so naive that he believed their love would last forever, and maybe it would have if Kylie hadn't gotten pregnant.

He'd even believed their relationship would be fine until she disappeared the day after she'd told him she was pregnant. No one would tell him anything. He'd asked her parents and Mira where she'd gone. He hadn't known whether they were lying to him or if they really didn't know, but no one had said anything helpful. It had taken him years to get over her. He'd dated, but he had never forgotten Kylie and had never stopped wondering about her and the baby he'd fathered—not until she'd shown up last summer and started dating Lance.

Seeing her had brought back all of his feelings for her, but he'd been able to tamp down his wish of reconciliation because of his anger at her for denying him the right to know anything about their child. When he'd learned the baby had been stolen from her as well, all he could feel was her pain.

Remembering how much he loved Kylie was why he'd been in Montana with Eva. Kylie was with Lance, and as much as Tom wanted to be with her, he respected that she was in love with Lance. All he wanted was for Kylie and Lance to be happy. He would just prefer it if they were happy with anyone other than each other.

Lance patted Tom's knee again and stood. "I'm off to bed. It's good to see you."

"I'm going to sit here for a while, maybe have another beer or two. My clock is still goofed up. Still on mountain time."

"Sure thing. Your room is down the hall. Second door on the left."

Tom sighed in relief when he was finally alone with his memories. He stared at the fire and didn't realize Lance had returned until his brother cleared his throat.

"What's up, little brother?" he asked, surprised to see the serious expression on Lance's face.

"Look, I don't know what you're doing here. If I'm wrong, I'm sorry, but I need to tell you that I love Kylie. You're welcome to stay here for a few days, but stay away from her."

"Stay away from her? How should I do that? It's her house."

"You know what I mean."

"No, I don't. You think I came here to steal your girlfriend from you?" He took a swallow of his beer. "You really think I'd do that?"

"I don't know you anymore. You seem to like getting a rise out of her and bringing up your past with her."

"Maybe you should worry more about yourself and the present instead of my past with her. If your relationship is so damned wonderful, you don't have anything to worry about. She has no reason to want anything from me and our past since she has you right now. Right?"

"It's great. You don't have any sort of chance."

Tom shook his head dismissively. "You don't have anything to worry about. I'm not here to steal Kylie from you. You're my brother. I'm glad you're happy. I'm glad Kylie's happy. However, I'm disappointed that you think so little of me, and Kylie for that matter. If she loves you, she loves you. Nothing I can do will change that, right?"

"Right." Lance glanced at the fireplace then met Tom's gaze. "You're right. I just wanted to make sure we understand each other."

"Perfectly." He hadn't come home to ruin Kylie's relationship with Lance. He just wanted to be around her. He wanted to make her laugh and smile like he used to.

Chapter 5

LANCE SLID INTO the bed next to Kylie and kissed her. "I love you."

She wrapped her arms around him and kissed him back. As much as she wanted her heart to race from feeling his lips on hers, it didn't happen. His kiss was comforting and made her feel safe. "I love you too." She'd been worried he would be upset and jealous of the past, but he seemed fine. "Did you get your brother all settled in?"

"He's still in the living room. I'd rather be tucked in with you, though."

She smiled against his shoulder, but when he cupped her breast through her oversized T-shirt, she rolled away. "Not tonight."

"Why not?"

"I'm just not interested. Besides, your brother is here."

He raised his head and adjusted his pillow. When he dropped his head, he crossed his arms over his chest and sighed. "You're not interested because he's here?"

She rubbed at her aching neck. "I'm not interested in having sex when anyone else is in my house." She turned back over and placed a hand on his arm, squeezing gently. "Look, I'm just stressed out about Christmas. I hate the holidays."

"Okay." Lance kissed her cheek and pulled the blanket up. "Sleep well."

"Yeah. Like that's going to happen," she muttered as she faced the patio door overlooking the lake. It was a lie. Although she really didn't like the holidays, that wasn't the reason she couldn't sleep. The truth was she just couldn't relax while Tom was in her house. She certainly couldn't relax and enjoy making love with Lance when he was downstairs.

Since she'd started dating Lance, she always felt awkward around Tom. She'd tried not to have a relationship with Lance when she returned to Chinkapin last summer to take care of her grandfather's estate, but he'd convinced her everything was fine. He'd claimed it didn't matter to him that she'd dated his brother. He'd even sworn it didn't upset him that she'd gotten pregnant while dating Tom.

She'd struggled to keep Lance from knowing how much Tom still affected her. Sometimes, she still wished everything had worked out with her and Tom, that they had gotten married and were raising Erick together. But that was just a fantasy now.

When her parents had sent her to Middleton to have her baby at fifteen, she'd believed everything would be okay. She had thought Tom would be happy to see her when she returned with their baby. Instead, she'd been told her son had died, and her parents had enrolled her at Interlochen Art Academy, a boarding school in Michigan. She'd sent a few letters to Tom, explaining what had happened, but they'd been returned unopened. When she returned to Chinkapin last summer, Tom had refused to even speak to her.

* * *

Around five the next morning, Kylie gave up trying to sleep. She went up to the attic studio to draw until her stomach started growling at seven. She set down the sketch she'd been working on. She'd drawn a fire in the fireplace downstairs and a couple in an embrace, covered by a patchwork quilt. The woman had her long curly red hair, but the man's face was turned away so no one knew who he was. Kylie wasn't even sure who she'd drawn.

On her way to the kitchen, she heard the toilet in the guest bathroom flush. She froze and turned back toward the stairs. She was about to ascend the stairs to her room when Tom stepped out of the bathroom.

"Morning," he said with a grin.

"Hey," she mumbled, grateful he was already dressed in jeans and a sweatshirt. "I was just going to find some breakfast. Hungry?"

"Sure."

She led the way to the kitchen, self-conscious of the boxers and T-shirt she wore.

"Lance said you did a bunch of remodeling. What was it?"

She started a pot of coffee while talking over her shoulder. "I combined a couple bedrooms to make a master suite and updated the kitchen, but you probably noticed that already. That's about it inside. I never got around to doing anything with the guest room. Sorry for the old bed."

"No problem. It beats staying with my parents, and it seemed silly to open up my house for just a week."

She nodded and cracked some eggs into a bowl. "No problem." Even though having him there was awkward as hell, she would never admit it to him. When she opened the fridge, she furrowed her forehead. The case of beer Lance had bought yesterday was gone. "Where did all the beer go?"

"Don't worry. I'll replace it today. I was hoping Lance would drive me over to my place so I could get my truck. That way, I don't have to depend on you guys to drive me around. Unless *you* want to drive me over there. We could go snowshoeing."

Kylie had always loved being outside, and snowshoeing was her favorite winter activity. She loved seeing everything pristine and covered with snow. Tom remembering how much she enjoyed it made it hard to breathe. "I have to run some errands today, but Lance or I can drop you off at your place."

"That would be great. You know, I meant that you, Lance, and I should go snowshoeing. Not just the two of us."

"Yeah, I suppose if Lance wants to, we can go."

Kylie cooked the scrambled eggs and set the bowl on the table along with a plate of toast, but she was still thinking about the beer. She'd had two beers. Lance was just opening his second when she went to bed. He seldom had more than three a night, but even if he'd had four, that still left eighteen. Zero remained. She poured the coffee and handed a mug to Tom. "Did you really drink a case of beer last night?"

"Of course not. Lance helped. So did you."

She kept her gaze on her plate and wondered how someone could drink that much beer and still seem perfectly normal the next morning. She made a mental note to talk to Lance about Tom's drinking. He'd never seemed like the type of person who would grow up to have a drinking problem, but life didn't always turn out as expected. She was proof of that.

They ate in silence, and as Kylie was finishing up, Lance

entered the kitchen and squeezed her shoulder on the way to the coffeepot. "What are you two doing up so early?"

"I've been upstairs drawing," Kylie replied. "I couldn't sleep. When I got hungry, I came down to start breakfast."

"I smelled coffee, so I got up," Tom said.

Kylie's gaze shifted from the table to Tom, as she wondered why he was lying. Tom looked toward the living room, and Kylie wondered if he was seeing memories instead of the furniture that she saw when she looked.

Lance opened the fridge to get some juice and let out a whistle. "Drinking and drawing, honey?"

Kylie shook her head. Drawing was her escape from reality. She had no need to drink as well as draw. "No."

Tom laughed. "I was thirsty. I'll restock the fridge for you guys."

Lance raised an eyebrow.

"What are your plans for the day? Tom wanted to know if one of us could give him a ride to his house so he could get his truck." Kylie hoped Lance would agree to drive his brother. Even though she'd agreed out of politeness, she wasn't ready to be alone with Tom in a vehicle. She wasn't even sure she was ready to go snowshoeing with him and Lance.

"Yeah. I have to run over to the station anyway this morning. I have an appointment to talk to the chief."

Kylie's eyebrows shot up, and she turned away. There hadn't been any mention of visiting the chief of police. No discussion of anything other than coming back for Christmas and the wedding.

Their personal belongings were still in the apartment in Traverse City. She'd planned on returning to Michigan in the middle of February, but now she wondered whether Lance had plans of returning to his job as a Chinkapin police officer.

"I'm going to take a shower." As she passed by Lance on her way out of the kitchen, he touched her arm, looking as though he intended to kiss her.

She didn't even bother trying to smile at him when she walked away. He scratched the side of his neck and let his hand drop from her arm as she moved out of the kitchen without looking at him again.

* * *

After Lance and Tom left in Lance's Jeep, Kylie drove to her parents' house. She expected her father to be at work and hoped she could have a nice visit with her mother. Or at least, she hoped for a non-hostile visit in which she might be able to learn more about where Erick was.

When her mother opened the door, surprise flashed across her face, but she smiled tentatively, smoothed her hands over her iron-gray hair, and invited Kylie in. They were settled at the kitchen table with cups of tea before her mother spoke. "How long have you been back? Hazel said you and Lance were living in Michigan."

Of course Lance's mother would tell Kylie's mother what she knew. Lance didn't seem to understand why Kylie didn't want to be best friends with her mom and dad. She just wanted to start mending the fences her parents had broken eleven years ago. "A couple days. Lance wanted to come back here for Christmas."

"And you?"

She took a sip of her tea. "I wanted to spend Christmas with him." There wasn't any reason to mention how miserable her previous Christmases had been. If her mother wanted to know, she would have asked.

Her mother ran her hands over the front of her blue-and-white floral T-shirt before speaking. "Are you happy, dear?"

"As happy as can be expected. I love Lance. We're good together." A week ago, she would have said they were great together, but with Lance, there had never been the instant desire when he touched her. Kylie frowned and shook her head. She wasn't supposed to be thinking about Tom right now. She wasn't supposed to think about Tom as anything more than an ex-boyfriend who happened to be Lance's brother.

"And Tom?"

It took a moment for Kylie to realize that her mother wasn't asking how she and Tom were together. "I think he's still pissed."

"Why?"

Kylie leaned back, confused at the question. "What do you mean 'why'?"

"Well, the same thing happened to you, and you're happy. Why can't Tom be happy? Hazel is so worried about him."

"I'm happy with Lance. That doesn't mean I'm happy about what you guys did to us. Have you forgotten that you kept me away from Tom by sending me to Middleton? And you helped his parents convince the school to lie about Erick passing away so some complete strangers could adopt and raise our son?"

"I've apologized. We all have."

Kylie stared into her teacup then took a deep breath. "I didn't come over here to fight."

"Why did you come over?" Her mother laughed shrilly. "I mean I'm glad you did. I'm just surprised and confused."

"I was curious about your plans for Christmas." Kylie couldn't bring herself to admit that she was hoping her family would invite her to join them. She wanted to have a normal Christmas. She really wanted to have a family, even if she was upset with her parents. If they would treat her as if they still loved her, she would be able to move forward. She may never forgive them for what they'd done, but they could work toward building a new relationship.

"We're going to midnight mass like always. We'll have dinner here on Christmas with Scott and the girl he's been seeing. Same as always. What are your plans?"

"I'm not sure. The Mallocks invited me and Lance over. I'm not sure if I'm going or not."

"You should go. I'm sure it'll be lovely."

Kylie frowned at her cup. The invitation she wanted didn't appear to be forthcoming this year either. It seemed that no matter how she tried to forgive the past and move on, her family just wasn't interested in being a family. "Who is Scott dating?"

After scratching the back of her head, her mother glanced around the room. "I can't remember her name. She's from Duluth."

Kylie nodded and stood. "Well, thanks for the tea. I have some grocery shopping to do before Lance gets home. Merry Christmas." She rushed from the house before she could start crying, but she had to stop her truck a couple of blocks away until her vision cleared.

Once she'd cried all of her tears, she drove to the bar where she'd heard her brother was working as a bartender. When she walked in, Scott looked up but didn't acknowledge her. He turned his back and leaned on the bar to talk to a brunette woman wearing a flannel shirt just as ratty as his.

Kylie stood by the bar, being ignored for a few minutes before another bartender approached. "What can I get you?"

The bartender must have been new to town because Kylie didn't recognize him at all. She gestured toward Scott. "Nothing to drink. I just want to talk to my brother."

"So go talk to him."

"If only life was so easy," she muttered, walking around the U-shaped bar to approach Scott and the woman. She slid onto the stool next to the woman and extended her hand. "Hi. I'm Kylie, Scott's sister."

Up close, she could see that the woman's hair was actually more of a purplish-burgundy than brown. The woman touched the silver stud in her right nostril then extended her hand. "Sunny." She glanced at Scott. "You didn't tell me you had a sister."

Scott swiped at the bar with a white rag. "We don't talk."

"Why not?" Sunny gestured at the beer mug in front of her. "Can I buy you a drink? You look like you could use one."

Kylie shook her head. "Thanks, but no. I just wanted to talk to Scott for a bit, find out what's new in his life."

Scott held Kylie's gaze for a few seconds then shook his head. "We don't have anything to talk about. Besides, I'm busy."

Kylie looked pointedly around the empty bar.

"Maybe some other time," Scott said.

Kylie nodded, unwilling to make a scene. "I'm at Grandpa's house until Mira's wedding. Stop over sometime."

"Yeah. Sure." Scott crossed his arms until she stood.

"Nice to meet you, Sunny. Maybe I'll see you around."

"That'd be great," Sunny replied, causing Scott to glower at both of them.

As soon as Kylie stepped away, she heard Sunny ask Scott what his problem was. After that, their voices were too muffled to hear over the regrets ringing in her ears.

"I'm so stupid. Why can't I just accept that they don't want to be a part of my life? It'd be less painful that way."

* * *

That evening, Tom, Lance, and Kylie were finishing dinner when Tom turned to Kylie. "Are you going to my parents' house on Christmas Eve?"

Kylie swallowed her last bite of roast beef and shrugged. "I haven't decided yet. Why?"

"Why not?" Lance asked.

"I think it would be uncomfortable, and I don't really like holidays."

"You said you'd go," Lance said.

"I said I'd probably go. I didn't make any promises."

Tom leaned back and grinned. "What could possibly be uncomfortable about a family function with your ex's parents?"

"My parents too." Lance shoved away from the table. "I really doubt it'll be that bad. It's not like you guys are still kids. Or even dating. What can they do? Besides, Mom invited you, Kylie. If she didn't want you there, why would she invite you?"

Kylie stood to clear the table as Lance ran dishwater. "Why is it such a big deal if I just stay here?"

"Great idea. Let's just stay here and drink." Tom flashed another grin, and Kylie's heart stopped.

She didn't really want to go to the Mallocks', but she definitely didn't want Tom hanging around her house on Christmas Eve, especially if Lance was at his parents'. She would feel obligated to put on a happy face and be pleasant. If she stayed home, she wanted to be alone to mope in solitude.

Lance faced her, leaning back to rest on the counter edge and tapping his foot on the gray ceramic tile. "If you don't want to go, I guess we can just stay home. I told you I wasn't going to let you have any more lonely Christmases."

Kylie gave a quick shake of her head, hoping Lance would understand that she didn't want to discuss this in front of Tom.

Tom carried his dishes to the sink and removed a towel from the drawer. "Lonely Christmases? What do you normally do on Christmas?"

"Nothing. Don't worry about it."

"She normally stays home," Lance said.

"What the hell for?"

Kylie forced a laugh, even though the reminder of how

little her family cared made her want to cry. "Haven't you noticed that I'm not close to my family? I haven't spent Christmas with them since I was fifteen."

"Their loss." Tom shook the towel at her. "Come on. Join us at our parents'. At least you won't be alone. Who knows, maybe our nieces and nephews will make you laugh. They're entertaining."

After trying and failing to swallow the lump in her throat, Kylie glanced at Lance, wondering why he hadn't mentioned his sisters' children. Christmas was hard enough for her. Kids would just remind her of everything she'd missed out on—and was still missing out on—with Erick being taken from her.

Lance shook his head and patted Kylie's hand. "It's nice. It'll be calm and quiet this year. Our sisters and their families won't be there."

Tom spun to look at Lance. "Why?"

"I don't know. I didn't ask for details." Lance met Kylie's gaze. "It's just dinner with Tom and my parents. No pressure. No strangers. No kids. No being alone."

"It'll be fine," Tom offered. "No one will make you feel uncomfortable. I'll make sure of it."

Lance rolled his eyes. "*We* will make sure of it, but you don't have anything to worry about. Our parents aren't uncivilized."

Kylie stared down at the table. Lance's comment made her wonder if he'd completely forgotten his parents had paid someone at Middleton to lie and say that Erick had died. Clearly, she hadn't been good enough for their son eleven years ago. She doubted that they had become more open-minded over the years. She didn't want to spend the evening biting her tongue and clenching her fists to keep from yelling at them.

Even though she questioned Lance's judgment on his parents, she really wanted to spend Christmas with him. So despite the little voice in her head whispering, "This is going to end badly," she nodded. "Okay."

Lance kissed her cheek. "I have some more good news."

Kylie wanted to ask what the first bit of good news was, but she kept quiet instead. If he believed that her agreeing to go to his parents' house was good news, so be it. "What's up?"

"The chief said I can start next week. He's been short-staffed since I left."

"What? You talked to him about a job?" Kylie turned away to open the cupboard, just for something to do other than clench her fists and scream like she wanted.

"Well, yeah. Why else would I have talked to the chief?"

"I thought you just wanted to stop in and BS with some of your old friends." She slammed the cabinet and turned toward him. "I guess I was wrong, and you just want to ruin Christmas."

Tom cleared his throat and dropped the dish towel on the counter. "I'm going to go do something."

In her anger, Kylie had forgotten Tom was there. "Don't bother. He probably wouldn't have even told me if you weren't here."

He gathered the dirty dishes from the table. "That's not true. I didn't see any sense in upsetting you before I knew if he'd let me come back."

"So you knew it'd piss me off, and you still did it?"

"Christ, Kylie. I didn't agree to anything. I just said he wanted me to come back because he was short-staffed."

Tom grabbed his coat from the hook by the door. "Nah. I don't think I'm a part of this."

Kylie bit her lip then met Lance's gaze. "Thanks for giving me any indication that you wanted to come back for good."

Lance set the dishes on the counter and started running water. "I had no idea you intended to run away forever. I figured as long as Tom wasn't in Chinkapin, you'd come back with me."

Tom raised an eyebrow but didn't say anything as he shoved his feet into his boots.

"Tom's not the reason I left Chinkapin. He has nothing to do with it."

Lance dropped the plates into the sink with a clatter. "Liar. He's at least ninety percent of the reason for everything you do."

She clenched her jaw and glanced over to see Tom's reaction. He kept his head down and let himself out of the house. For a split second, she considered leaving too—not to be with Tom, but to get away from this conversation that rang a bit too true. Instead, she faced Lance. "That's not fair. Your past affects you too. That's not even the point. I thought we were serious, and you decided to stay here without telling me."

"I haven't decided anything. Besides, even if I do stay, you don't have to."

"Don't have to? Or you don't want me to?" She held her breath waiting for his response, hoping he wouldn't say he didn't want her with him.

"Don't be ridiculous." He moved closer and wrapped his arms around her stiff body. "Of course I want to be with you. I'm tired of not having a job, though. I like it here, and I'd like to live here."

Kylie kept herself rigid, refusing to relax against him. She'd suspected he wasn't happy in Michigan, but she hadn't anticipated this. "Why didn't you tell me?"

"I didn't see any sense in rocking the boat if the chief wasn't going to give me my job back."

"Talking to each other is part of being in a relationship. Don't you think you could have at least told me in private?"

Lance kissed the corner of her mouth, and as her anger dissipated, she shifted closer to him. "I'm sorry. Next time I have big news I'll tell you in private, okay?"

"Thank you," she whispered as she hugged him.

"Would it really be so bad to stay here? It's different this time. We're together now. I know you've missed the house."

"Yes, I've missed the house." But she hadn't missed being treated poorly by her family and other people around town who remembered she hadn't attended her younger sister's funeral. "I'm not sure I want to come back permanently, though."

"Why?"

"You just don't get it, Lance. Your past here is happy. Your memories are happy. Mine aren't. I've been an outcast for years. Everywhere I look, I see people that know my parents and/or your parents, and I wonder if they know where Erick is. The only place around here that I ever relax is upstairs in my studio."

"You need to let go of the past and move on."

Kylie backed away. "You are completely blind, Lance. It's not that easy to let go."

He crossed his arms. "So if I accept the job, are you going

to stay?"

She stared down at the floor then wrapped her arms around herself. "I don't know."

He reached for her. "Come on, Kylie. Isn't our relationship more important than where we live?"

She moved back two more steps. "Is it?" When he didn't answer, she turned and left the room.

Chapter 6

"WHERE DID YOU disappear to last night?" Lance asked Tom as he sat down at the kitchen table with his mug the next morning.

"I went to the bar for a bit."

Lance glanced at the trash can full of aluminum cans. "Then drank another case of beer when you got back?"

"I couldn't sleep. It tasted good. No harm, no foul, right?" Tom didn't see anything wrong with finishing off the beer. He didn't have a job to get to, he didn't drive anywhere, and he was perfectly fine this morning. He hadn't expected an inquisition about drinking it when he'd opened the fridge. For a few seconds, he wondered what Lance would say if he admitted why he'd drunk all the beer.

Last night, he'd had a few beers at the bar with Keefe before coming back here and going to bed. Once he was lying in the guest room, his imagination ran amok with images of Kylie, his memories combining with the strange house. Every single noise made him wonder whether or not Kylie and Lance were asleep, whether they slept wrapped around one another or hugging their respective sides of the bed.

When he started imagining different sleepwear for Kylie, he'd gotten out of bed and raided the fridge. He knew there was zero chance of sleeping, so he'd drunk until he was about to pass out.

Lance shrugged. "Sure."

"So you're after your old job, huh? I thought you guys were happy in Michigan."

Lance took a piece of cold toast from the plate and bit into it. "We are."

"You know, from the look on Kylie's face when you mentioned it, I'd guess she had no idea you were going to look for a job while you were here."

"What's it matter to you? You're leaving in a few days."

"You think that's going to make it easier for her to stay here?" It may have been years since Tom had had a real heartfelt conversation with Kylie, but he'd picked up on her resistance to being in Chinkapin. He'd been surprised that she'd stayed in town long enough last summer to fall for Lance, but maybe falling for Lance was the reason she'd stayed.

"You don't know anything about Kylie anymore."

"I know we're going snowshoeing. You're invited too, of course." He didn't want to invite Lance, but he doubted Kylie would go with just him.

Lance narrowed his eyes at Tom. "Why do you want to go snowshoeing?"

"Why not? Are you afraid that Kylie is going to have fun?"

"I assumed you were going to visit our parents."

"I will. Just not today." He finished his coffee. "So are you coming with us?"

Lance frowned. "I can't. I have another meeting with the chief today."

Tom pushed back from the table and carried his dishes to the sink. He ran hot water so he could wash the breakfast dishes. "Does that mean Kylie agreed to stay in Chinkapin?"

"Not yet, but she'll come around."

Tom nodded, hiding his smile. If Kylie's world shattered because of Lance's decision to accept the job offer, Tom intended to pick up the pieces. Something told him life wasn't all leprechauns and rainbows for Kylie and Lance. That gave him hope.

* * *

Tom stumbled over his snowshoe tip and grabbed at the pine boughs to prevent himself from face-planting in the drifts. Regaining his balance, he cursed under his breath then rubbed at his thigh.

"You okay?" Kylie asked from behind him.

"Yep. Fine. Do you want to go ahead of me?" If she was in front, she wouldn't see him stumbling like a newborn colt.

"I'm fine with you setting the pace."

Surely, she didn't mean to sound condescending or patronizing, but her worried tone caused his heart to race and sweat to bead on his forehead. Her concern didn't bother him nearly as much as his uncooperative leg, which really pissed him off. His leg was as good as the doctors could make it. All he could do was keep exercising. The stronger it was, the less trouble it would give him.

He could walk normally on a smooth floor. Icy sidewalks were horrible. Snowshoeing was an idiotic idea, but Kylie loved winter and doing stuff outside in the snow. He took it as a positive sign that she'd come with him even after Lance bowed out. He glanced over his shoulder at her.

"Do you mind if we take a break?" she asked. "I wore new boots, and they're starting to bother my feet."

He suspected she was making excuses for his benefit, but at that point, he needed a break. He pointed at a fallen tree. "We can sit there."

"Great." Kylie trudged over to the tree and brushed the fluffy snow from it before sitting down. She pulled off her backpack and removed a thermos. "Coffee?"

"Sure." Tom broke a few twigs and lowered himself next to her on the log. He took the thermos and twisted the top off. Steam wafted over his fingers as he poured the dark-brown liquid into the cup. He held it out to her, and she shook her head.

She removed her snowshoes and untied her bootlaces. "Go ahead. I need to fix these boots."

"You don't have to pretend." Tom inhaled deeply, savoring the scented steam before he took a swallow of the coffee.

"Really? You think I'd bother pretending to make you feel better about something?" She slid her boot off and adjusted her wool sock before replacing the boot. "You're an adult, not a stupid kid, Tom. If you needed a break, you'd tell me." She faced him. "Wouldn't you?"

He nodded, stricken by her red cheeks and nose. Her face was relaxed and calm. She looked wonderful, and he wanted to kiss her for treating him as though he could take care of himself. He wondered if her lips would warm beneath his. She used to be willing to kiss him for hours.

Once her boots were retied, she tugged her knit cap lower and grinned at him. He could barely believe eleven years had passed since their relationship. Other than the wrinkles at the corners of her eyes, she looked the same as she had when he'd first seen her sketching near the river.

He refilled the aluminum cup and held it out to her, and she removed her mittens before reaching for it. Their fingers brushed, and he was surprised at the warmth emitting from her.

Instead of letting go of the cup, he caressed her fingers. He knew he shouldn't enjoy it as much as he did, yet he couldn't pull away.

Kylie yanked her hand back, and the coffee spilled over both of their hands.

"Shit," he muttered. "That's hot."

"Coffee's supposed to be hot. Isn't it?" Kylie set the cup down and stuck her hand in the snow. Her grin didn't reach her eyes as she removed her knit cap and wiped her hand with it before putting her mittens back on. "Ready to go?"

"Hang on. Let me take a look at that."

She shook her head and stood. "I'm fine. I've been burned before."

Unwilling to let her leave, he grabbed her arm and tugged her back to sit next to him. He peeled her mitten off to reveal an angry red patch on the back of her hand. "That's going to blister."

She pulled, but he didn't let go. "I'll be fine."

"Sit still. I have a first aid kit in my pack." He shrugged out of the backpack and set it between his feet. "Let's get some snow on that first."

He removed his gloves and held a handful of loosely packed snow on the back of her hand.

"Come on, Tom. It's fine. Let's just go."

He ignored her words and focused on the feel of her skin against his. The longer he held her hand, the less the world mattered to him. He didn't care that he struggled to walk or that she was dating his brother. Happiness seemed to be draped around them. After a few minutes, he could feel her relax next to him. "Does it hurt?"

"Not too bad." Her voice was softer than normal, and when he looked up from her hand, she was staring at him.

"You okay?" he asked.

She nodded then caught her lower lip between her teeth, reminding him of how she used to nip at his lips when they made love. He held her gaze for a few seconds as his heart raced.

When she released her lip from her teeth and ran her tongue over it, he swallowed hard and shifted on the fallen log as his jeans became uncomfortably tight.

"Tom," she whispered and brought her unburned hand up to touch his cheek as she leaned toward him.

Even though he wanted nothing more than to lean forward and kiss her, he released her hand and dug through his pack to fish out the first aid kit. "It's not that great of a kit, but it's better than nothing. I have some burn ointment, and we can bandage it up. At least it won't be rubbing on the inside of your mitten."

When she didn't respond, he selected a roll of gauze and a tube of medicated ointment. "It even says it helps with pain. Does it hurt?"

She shook her head mutely, still staring at him.

"So what happened last night after I left?" he asked as he gently spread ointment over the back of her hand.

"What do you mean?"

"Is Lance taking the job?"

She shrugged and shifted her gaze to their hands. "I don't know."

"If he does, are you going to stay?" He deftly wrapped her hand with gauze then zipped his pack but didn't stand. He wanted to sit there, next to Kylie and talk about nothing and everything of importance. If he was being honest, he wanted to kiss her until the snow melted around them. He wanted to grab her hand and run the half mile through the woods to his house and fall into bed with her. Instead, he sat still, hands clasped loosely between his knees.

"I don't know."

He watched a gray squirrel run across a branch thirty feet away, causing clumps of snow to fall from the Norway pine. "I guess you didn't know what he was doing?"

"No. I never would have…" She brought her hand to her face and turned away from him.

"Never would have what?" he asked, watching the squirrel.

She shook her head. "I should have just sold Grandpa's house last summer. I shouldn't have come back. I shouldn't have started dating him."

Tom jerked his gaze back to her. "Why not? Aren't you guys happy?"

"I thought so, but he wants to live here. I'm not sure I can."

"So what are you going to do? Dump him just because of where he wants to live? That seems harsh. You guys really do seem happy." He held his breath, hoping she would deny their happiness.

"Maybe it is a little drastic. I don't know what I'm going to do."

"Do you love him?"

She cocked her head and rolled her eyes but wouldn't hold his gaze. "What do you think?"

Tom ducked his head to hide his grin over the fact that things weren't perfect between Kylie and Lance. "I think if you loved him, you'd be trying to figure out how to make it work instead of looking for an excuse to cut bait and run."

"It's not quite that easy. It's not easy being here."

"Why? Because people are immature and blame you for something you had no control over years ago? Or because all your memories of Chinkapin are bad?"

She shook her head and fixed her gaze on the snow between her purple snow boots. "They're not all bad."

"The people or the memories?"

She grinned at him, and he smiled back. "Neither." She let out a big sigh. "I just can't believe he didn't tell me. I thought we were closer than that."

Tom shifted enough to bump his shoulder against hers. "It'll be okay." The way she'd looked at him a few minutes ago made it clear that she wasn't one hundred percent convinced her relationship with Lance was the one she wanted to be in.

"Yeah, you're probably right." Again, her smile didn't reach her eyes.

He watched her from the corner of his eye for a couple of minutes before she spoke again. "What's with you and Eva?"

Caught off guard by her question, he had to clear his throat a couple of times before he could speak. "Why?"

"Why didn't she come with you?"

He hadn't even thought of Eva since they'd parted ways at the airport. "She had other plans." Contemplating whether to tell her that he was tired of Eva, he reached over and squeezed her mitten-covered hand. "Besides, how would I lure you away from Lance if Eva was here too?"

Her eyebrows shot up, and she tried to pull away, but he held on. "I'm kidding."

Kylie nodded with a serious look on her face. "We should head back."

"Tired of my company already?"

She laughed and stood before fastening her snowshoes and turning toward home without answering his question.

Chapter 7

THAT EVENING, KYLIE, Lance, and Tom were sitting in the living room watching the evening news after supper. Tom cleared his throat, and Kylie looked up from the magazine she was paging through to glance at him.

"I thought I'd let you guys know that tonight's the last night I'll be here."

Lance lowered the volume of the television. "What? Tomorrow's Christmas Eve. I thought you were going to Mom and Dad's. Isn't that why you came back from Montana?"

Kylie nodded at Lance's comment even though she wished she could leave town too. She'd been considering heading back to Michigan since Lance admitted he wanted to stay in Chinkapin, but she wasn't going to bail right before Christmas, especially when it was the first Christmas she wouldn't be alone. There was still a chance that Lance would change his mind. "Yeah, why are you leaving? You and Lance begged me to go over there, and now you're skipping out on it?"

Tom shook his head. "I'm not leaving town. I'm just not going to be staying here. Tomorrow morning, I'm going back to my house."

Kylie frowned. "There's plenty of room. There's no sense in opening up your house for just a couple days."

"No, I'm staying."

Lance smiled. "You mean you're not going back to Montana?"

Kylie dropped her gaze to the magazine in her lap. It was bad enough that Lance wanted to stay in Chinkapin. Now Tom was staying too. A part of her wondered if he was staying because he really was trying to lure her away from Lance. She'd almost convinced herself that she and Lance could be fine in Chinkapin once the holidays had passed, but if Tom was living there again, she didn't know how things would go. Their near kiss while snowshoeing was a perfect example of what she feared would happen any time she was alone with Tom.

"What about Eva?" she asked without looking up from her magazine.

Tom didn't answer until she looked up at him, then he shook his head. "Eva and I aren't serious. Never have been."

"Does she know that?"

Lance's chuckle drew her attention.

"What's so funny?"

"You're defending Eva?" Lance asked.

"I'm not defending anyone. I just asked a question. Does Eva know that living with Tom for months and helping him get back on his feet is nothing?"

Tom grinned. "Eva knows that we're not getting married or having kids together. We're adults who enjoyed one another's company. Now it's time to move on."

"Why?" Kylie's stomach sank. She'd hoped Tom would have a real reason for ending it with Eva.

Lance peered at her. "Why so much interest in Tom and Eva's relationship?"

She turned her attention back to the magazine and forced her fingers to relax until the pages lay flat again. "You're right. It's none of my business. I'm sure your family will be glad you're staying in Minnesota instead of going back to Montana."

"I'm sure." The sarcasm practically dripped from his words.

Lance raised his beer toward Tom. "To coming home."

Tom raised his glass in return, and Kylie nodded.

"To coming home," she mumbled as she stood and forced a smile. "I'm beat. I'll see you guys in the morning." Without waiting for a response, she walked upstairs to her room.

Still awake an hour later, she rose from the bed and pulled a sweatshirt over the T-shirt and boxers she'd been sleeping in since Tom had been visiting. As she reached for the door, it opened. Lance stepped in, grinned, and pressed his mouth to hers. Instead of kissing him back, though, she pulled away. She doubted the rationality of them returning to Chinkapin.

"What's going on?" Lance asked. "Ever since Tom has been here, you've been acting strange."

"He's my ex-boyfriend. It's weird having him around, and he's your brother. We talked about this."

"So? I thought you'd be over it by now."

"So, I don't want to be around him, but I don't want to come between the two of you."

"You don't want to be around him, yet you went snowshoeing with him."

She took a deep breath and stared at the window. She couldn't see anything other than the reflection of their room. Lance stood behind her, staring at the back of her head with a look of concern. She couldn't tell him that she missed what she'd had with Tom. She missed the carefree feeling of being in love for the first time. It wasn't necessarily better than what she had with Lance; it was just different.

"I did. Is that a problem?" Before he could respond, she tried to lighten the mood. "You were invited. What's the big deal, anyway? Don't you trust us?" she joked. She nearly missed him pressing his lips together for a fraction of a second before he smiled and shook his head.

"Don't be ridiculous. Of course I trust you."

"Good. Because you don't have any reason not to trust us. Or to worry about anything. I love you." She wrapped her arms around him and snuggled against him, trying to feel happy, but that was impossible when she knew he didn't trust her.

Lance hugged her back, and she wished she felt something other than contentment. She knew they needed to talk about his job offer, and she knew if she wanted to remain in a relationship with him, she would have to accept that he wanted to live in Chinkapin. Right now, though, she didn't want to think about any of it. She just wanted them to be back in their crappy little apartment in Michigan where they laughed and joked and had sex wherever they felt like it.

He nuzzled the side of her neck, almost as if he could read her mind. "What are you doing up? I thought you were tired."

"I am, but I can't sleep. I was on my way upstairs to draw."

He slid his hands down her arms and winked. "I bet I can help you relax."

She fought back her grimace and smiled. Maybe having sex with Lance was just what she needed to get Tom out of her mind.

As he pressed her back into the bed, she bent her knees and

pulled him down on top of her. Twining his hands through her hair, he angled his mouth over hers, and she forced her thoughts to focus on him and his touch. His hand slid down the side of her neck, followed by his mouth as he kissed her pulse.

Instead of being swept away by him, she found herself wondering what would have happened if she had kissed Tom in the woods. Would he have kissed her back? Would it have been everything she thought it would, or would she have been just as disappointed as she'd been with Lance's kisses this past week?

"You know, we don't have to do the whole 'foreplay thing' tonight," she whispered. "We can just have sex."

"I kinda like the whole 'foreplay thing.'"

"I normally do too, but like I said, I'm tired."

He raised his head and glared at her. "You just said you couldn't sleep."

"Right, and then we agreed that maybe having sex would help me relax. So let's have sex."

"You're not into this at all, are you?"

She sighed. "If I wasn't into it, I wouldn't be lying here with you. I just don't want you to put a lot of effort into it and be disappointed if I don't have an orgasm. So, let's just have sex and hope for the best."

He rolled away. "What exactly would be 'the best'?"

"That we both are pleased and can sleep." She glanced at the red digital clock. It'd been twelve minutes since she'd decided to go upstairs to draw, and ten minutes since they'd landed on the bed.

He rose and spoke as he walked into the bathroom. "Forget it. I'm not in the mood now."

"Come on, Lance. I'm trying."

He spun around and peeled off his T-shirt to reveal his muscular chest and abs. "That's just it. I don't want you to have to try. I want you to want me."

"Why can't me trying be enough? You can't expect us both to be in the mood every single time one of us is."

"I didn't say it wasn't enough. I said I'm not in the mood anymore."

As he shut the bathroom door calmly behind him, Kylie

rose from the bed and straightened her clothes. "We shouldn't have come back to Chinkapin," she muttered, heading upstairs to the attic before he came back into the bedroom.

Chapter 8

TOM LET HIMSELF into his parents' house on Christmas Eve. Dinner was supposed to be in an hour, but he'd decided it would be best if he arrived earlier and tried to talk things over with his parents, at least a little bit.

When he walked into the kitchen, he stood next to the sink for a minute. His mom looked older and tired. She shouldn't look that much older. It had only been three months since he'd seen her in Montana, yet there were lines on her face that he'd never noticed before.

She turned from the stove, holding a wooden spoon in her hand. When she saw Tom, she pressed her other hand to the chest of her red sweater. "Tom!" A second later, she tossed the wooden spoon on the counter and wrapped her arms around him. "I'm so glad you're home."

Even though he was angry with her, he still relaxed and took a deep breath when she hugged him. It didn't seem to matter what had happened in the past, her hug still comforted him the same way it always had. He fought to remain distant but couldn't.

She patted his back and moved away sooner than he would have liked, but his parents had never been demonstrative. "How long are you in town? Are you staying for good?"

"I haven't decided exactly. I'm here now, though." He intended to stay as long as Kylie was in town.

She picked up the spoon and turned back to the stove to stir the pot of simmering gravy. "When did you get here?"

"A few days ago. I've been staying with Kylie and Lance."

She stopped stirring for a few seconds, but when she spoke again, her voice was normal. "I'm so glad they came home for Christmas. I hope we can all put the past behind us and get back to being a family."

"Where's Dad?"

"He took the dogs for a walk down by the river. They

should be back any time."

"Oh." He looked around the kitchen. It was the same as it had been since he was little—dark-cherry cabinets, gray stone tile, top-of-the-line appliances. He remembered sitting right here, in junior high, confiding in his mother about the kids teasing him for being a Mallock. He and his mom used to be close. Maybe if he just asked her what he wanted to know, she would tell him. "Mom, whose idea was it to lie to Kylie and I?"

"Oh, honey." She spoke in her soothing manner, not as if she was trying to evade the question but just because she didn't want him to be upset by the topic. "Do you really want to talk about this now? Is it going to be easier for you if you have someone to blame? Do you need one specific person instead of the four of us?"

"I just want to know the truth." Tom rubbed the back of his neck then exhaled. Kylie and Lance would be there soon, and he'd promised Kylie that it wouldn't be uncomfortable if she joined them for dinner. "Okay. You're right. Let's not do this now. Let's enjoy Christmas Eve, and we can get together in a few days and deal with this. Does that sound better?"

"That sounds wonderful, dear. What do you think of Lance's big news?"

Tom froze. "What big news?"

"He's proposing to Kylie tonight. Didn't he tell you?"

No! Tom shoved away from the counter he'd been leaning against and yanked open the fridge. "Do you have any beer?"

"I'm sure there's some in there somewhere. Or there might be some upstairs in the game room fridge."

He shoved the refrigerator door shut and took the stairs two at a time up to the game room. Lance couldn't propose to Kylie. What if Kylie accepted? Tom had to tell Kylie how he felt about her before she could make such a decision. Except he couldn't tell Kylie how he felt. If she chose him over Lance, Lance would be devastated, and he doubted that Kylie would choose him. But that almost kiss…

He hadn't been able to think of anything since she'd nearly kissed him. She was why he'd decided to stay in Chinkapin. If she asked him to leave Chinkapin, he would pack his belongings in an instant. There was nothing in the town that he wanted more than he wanted to be with Kylie and Erick.

"Thomas, your father is back."

Tom fought the urge to punch the cream-colored wall in front of him. He didn't bother opening the fridge before turning and descending the stairs into the living room. Beer wasn't going to cut it tonight. He was going to need something much stronger in order to congratulate Lance and Kylie on their upcoming nuptials.

"Please, God. If you really exist, don't let him propose to her here. Not in front of me. I don't think I could handle it," he whispered as he strode across the room to pour himself a large glass of whiskey.

Chapter 9

KYLIE FOLLOWED LANCE into his parents' house. She just wanted to get through dinner and go home. Her heart had skipped a beat when they pulled into the driveway. She told herself it was just nerves about seeing the Mallocks, not because of Tom's red Ford truck in front of the garage.

She was grateful their sisters and families weren't going to be there. It would be hard enough to be pleasant toward Gil and Hazel Mallock. But Lance wanted to spend Christmas Eve with his parents, and Kylie wanted him to be happy. She also thought if they did what he wanted on Christmas Eve, they would do what she wanted on Christmas Day. So there they were.

They greeted the Mallocks, and Kylie complimented Hazel on her reindeer sweater, while Gil poured eggnog into cups covered with snowmen.

She forced herself to smile as she took the cup from him. "It's nice that you coordinated your sweater with the eggnog cups."

Gil tipped his head back to laugh then straightened the tie beneath his cardigan. "Anything to make my darling wife happy."

Unwilling to like him, Kylie nodded and reminded herself that these people had ruined her life. Even as she tried to hate them, she envied them. They were clearly still in love as they sank into matching armchairs and clasped hands. As Gil spoke to Lance, Hazel gazed at him adoringly.

Kylie settled onto the white couch with Lance and her mug of eggnog. Tom lounged on another white couch across from them on the opposite side of the room, as Kylie smoothed her dress and plucked a long gold hair from the couch beside her.

She gazed at the stone fireplace as Lance chatted with his parents about his intent to stay in Chinkapin. As his parents happily exclaimed how great it would be to have him home, she glanced at Tom.

He seemed as uncomfortable as Kylie felt, so she smiled. He caught her eye and grimaced before she turned her attention back to the crackling fire. The more she looked at him and saw him suffering, the more her heart twisted in her chest. Daydreaming about Tom wasn't going to make her fantasy Christmas with Lance come true. Getting through the night was the last hurdle before spending all of the next day cuddling with Lance on the couch in front of their tree.

After a while, her gaze shifted to the mantel, where family pictures were displayed. Her stomach twisted at the pictures of the entire family laughing and smiling. She didn't have happy memories of family vacations.

Even before she'd gotten pregnant at fifteen, Kylie had felt out of place, almost as if she wasn't even a part of the family. Neither of her parents understood her or even seemed to try.

Her siblings, Kristy and Scott, had been the best part of her family. Once Kylie met Tom, though, she'd spent less and less time with her brother and sister. By the time she learned Kristy had died of pneumonia while Kylie was at Middleton, she had felt like an orphan.

She shook her head to clear the memories and tried to focus on the conversation. When there was a lull, she said, "Tom's staying in Chinkapin too."

Gil and Hazel exchanged an astonished look, then Hazel brushed her short wavy silver hair back from her forehead. "That's wonderful, dear. Learning both my boys will be home again is the best Christmas gift."

Tom drained his highball glass of amber liquid, stood, and moved to the bar to refill it. Once it was full, he drank it without setting the crystal decanter down.

As he refilled the glass again, Lance asked, "What's the rush with getting drunk? Why can't you wait until you get home? Drink yourself into oblivion there instead of here."

"What difference does it make?"

"No one wants to see you drunk, especially on Christmas Eve."

"I don't really care what anyone wants."

"Why are you being an asshole?"

"No one has ever asked what I want. Why is that?"

Right now, Kylie wished she'd stayed home. Home alone would have been a million times better than getting stuck at the Mallocks with Tom getting drunk. He must have been even more miserable than she'd thought if he was so determined to be wasted tonight with his family. Kylie swallowed and leaned forward as she realized that Tom might not be able to control how much and when he drank.

"What the hell are you talking about?" Lance shifted his gaze from Tom to his parents, then to Kylie. "Do you know what he's talking about?"

Kylie rose from the sofa, resenting Lance questioning her about Tom's behavior. "I think I need a beer." She didn't want to get into a fight about Erick with the Mallocks, especially on Christmas Eve.

"Yeah. Grab me one too," Tom called as she went to the kitchen.

After getting two bottles of Heineken from the kitchen fridge, she peeked back into the living room. Gil stood in the corner, rubbing his forehead, and Hazel sat in a green armchair next to her husband, twisting beads of some sort in her lap as her lips moved. *A rosary? Really? She's Catholic, and she helped someone steal my son? Unbelievable.*

Lance and Tom were squared off in the center of the room when Kylie returned. She held a bottle of beer toward Tom.

Tom grinned and reached for it. "Thanks." His hand brushed over hers before he gripped the neck of the bottle.

Swallowing, Kylie stepped back even though she wanted to grab his hand and run from the room. She'd never liked bullies, and right now, it seemed as though Tom's entire family wanted nothing more than to bully him on the one night she thought families—other than hers—wanted to be together.

She lowered herself to the couch and sank back into the cushions before gulping her beer. If her family treated her like Tom's was treating him, she would probably develop a drinking problem too. It was hard to believe she had thought she wanted to spend Christmas with her family no matter what. Right now, it was clear that both she and Tom would have been better off never returning to Chinkapin for Christmas.

"What's your problem?" Lance asked Tom as he returned to Kylie's side on the couch.

"Are you still upset about your kid?" Gil asked.

Kylie glared at Gil. "His name is Erick. If you hadn't stolen him from us, you'd know that. Actually, you probably wouldn't know that. You're too self-centered to bother knowing anyone's name."

"Kylie!" Lance scowled at her and gave a little shake of his head.

"Don't we have a right to be pissed? You stole our son." Tom drained his glass again then set it on the mantel forcefully before taking a swallow of beer.

Gil cleared his throat and ran his hand over his head. "Is there any chance we cannot do this today?"

"Yeah, can't we just enjoy each other's company on Christmas Eve?" Lance asked.

She kept her eyes on the coffee table in front of her. She had plenty to say about their involvement with Erick's adoption, but she really didn't want to ruin Lance's Christmas. She nodded and reached for Lance's hand.

He shifted away so subtly that Kylie wondered if she had imagined it.

"Why?" Tom demanded with a glare. "Just so you guys can have a pleasant Christmas? What about me? Hell, what about Kylie? How many Christmases has she enjoyed since you stole our son?"

Kylie's head snapped up to look at Tom. She hadn't expected him to make the connection between her feelings about the holiday and missing Erick. Everyone looked at her as she swallowed.

"What?" Lance asked.

"You seriously think that not having Erick hasn't affected her? Christ, Lance, you're supposed to be the smart brother."

"I guess—"

"You're so worried about what they"—Tom pointed at his parents—"want, that you're completely blind to what Kylie wants."

"That's not true." Lance turned to Kylie, his eyebrows drawn together. "You said you wanted to come."

Kylie stared at Tom, realizing he was as upset about not having the chance to know Erick as she was. Her voice was barely above a whisper when she finally answered. "I said I wanted to be with you."

"Why did you agree if you don't want to be here? Why didn't you just say 'no'?"

Kylie cleared her throat, but before she could say anything, Tom spoke again.

"Because you're a selfish ass who has no clue what it's like to know your son is out there somewhere with people you don't know, doing God knows what. All because of our controlling parents, who only care about themselves and money. You're just like them."

Kylie frowned. While Lance wasn't perfect, she would never say he was just like his parents. She couldn't imagine Lance doing what their parents had done.

"That's enough." Gil held a hand up toward Tom in a "stop" gesture. "We did what we thought was best, and we've apologized."

Tom jerked away. "I'm leaving. I can't sit here and pretend everything is fine. Not when they"—he pointed at Gil and Hazel—"took it upon themselves to sell my child and lie about it."

Hazel pressed her lips together, raised her hand, and shooed Tom toward the door. "I think that's best."

Gil turned toward Lance. "Can you drive your brother home?"

Kylie glanced at Lance. "You can stay. I'll drive him home." It would give her a reason to leave, and Lance wouldn't be forced to leave his parents' house. Both Kylie and Lance could have what they wanted for the night.

Lance narrowed his eyes before shaking his head. "No, I'll do it. Let's go."

She resented being told what to do, but she wasn't going to argue. At least they were leaving.

Lance rose from the couch. "Let's go, Tom."

"Will you be back?" Hazel asked Lance.

He held Kylie's gaze as he spoke to his mother. "Not tonight."

Hazel dabbed a tissue at the corner of her eye. "My first Christmas without you guys."

Tom glared at his mother from where he held the door open. "And Kylie's and my eleventh without our son. Think on that."

Kylie took a deep breath. She hadn't expected Tom to be angry on her behalf. She'd thought he would just focus on his own mistreatment, but he was still looking out for her feelings. After all these years and knowing she was dating his brother, Tom was the one who truly cared and understood how she felt about Christmas.

"Let it go, Tom," Lance muttered.

"See how festive she is and then tell me to let it go." Tom yanked the door shut behind him. The happy tinkling of the bells on the wreath were completely out of place with the argument and anger in the room.

Kylie grabbed her coat, shoved her feet into her boots, and followed Tom. It wasn't how she'd expected the night to go. She'd expected to feel awkward and uncomfortable the entire night, but she hadn't expected a full-fledged fight about her and Erick.

When Tom opened the passenger door of the Jeep and flipped the seat forward so Kylie could get in the back, she met his gaze. His eyes glistened, and she lifted her hand as a tear slipped out of his eye. He clenched his jaw, shook his head, and gestured for her to get in the vehicle as she reached for him.

She turned away and got into the Jeep, wondering if she'd imagined the connection she'd felt to Tom. It was all she could do not to weep at her own loss on the ride. The tension was palpable as none of them spoke.

A couple of miles before they reached Tom's driveway, she felt a touch on her lower leg near the passenger door. From the way her nerves jangled and her body heated instantly, she knew it wasn't something accidental. It was Tom reaching around the side of the seat. She shifted in her seat so she could lay her hand on his. For the first time in eleven years on Christmas Eve, she felt peace. That peace was quickly displaced by a tightening in her abdomen as he brushed his fingertips up and down on her leg. His touch made her wish she hadn't worn tights so there was nothing between her skin and his.

When Lance slowed to turn into the driveway, she pulled away from Tom and tucked her hands into her pockets, reminding herself she wasn't there to reconcile with Tom.

She'd come back to Chinkapin because of Lance. All she wanted for Christmas was to spend the next day with Lance. Tom got out of Lance's Jeep and frowned. "Merry Fucking Christmas, huh?"

Lance ducked his head and glared at him through the open passenger door. "If that's not how you wanted Christmas to go, why did you bring it up?"

"Because I'm tired of pretending that everything is okay. It's not okay." Tom sighed and scratched his chin. "Sorry. Do you guys want to come in?"

Lance shifted the Jeep into reverse. "I just want to go home."

Tom touched Kylie's arm as she got out of the backseat to move to the front. "What about you? Want to spend Christmas Eve getting drunk with me and forgetting?" He laughed as he said it, but the laughter didn't make it to his eyes.

Kylie thought his expression of misery must match her own. She considered the possibility of drinking the past away then shook her head. Commiserating with Tom and booze wasn't a good idea. She knew if she had a few drinks and they touched, she wouldn't be able to stop herself. Her reaction to his touch a few minutes ago had proven that. "Thanks, but no."

Tom shrugged. "Your choice."

As Kylie slid into the front seat and buckled her seat belt. Tom grinned at Lance. "See how I did that? I asked her if she wanted to do something, and she said 'no.' I accepted her answer instead of cajoling her into doing something she didn't want to do."

As Lance pulled out of Tom's driveway, he shot her a glare. "What the hell was that supposed to mean? I listen to you. I don't cajole you to do things. Do I?"

She stared out the window. "Sometimes." He hadn't begged her to come back to Minnesota, but at that moment, it didn't feel as though she'd made that decision on her own.

He clenched his jaw. "I do not. He's just jealous."

"Of what?"

"Me living with you."

She reached for his hand, hoping to neutralize the situation before they got home. Tonight, they would be alone in her house, and if he wasn't being a jerk, she could easily be interested in showing him how much she loved him. "Are you drunk? He doesn't want to live with me. We mean nothing to one another." She rubbed her thumb over the back of his hand then froze when she realized it was the same motion Tom had made on her leg.

"Yeah, right. If you didn't mean anything to him, he wouldn't have done what he did."

She swallowed. Lance couldn't know that Tom had rubbed her leg. "You mean calling your parents on their behavior? Tom can't just be upset about what they did without being madly in love with me? Don't you think he has a right to be angry with them?"

"He needs to get over it before it destroys our family."

"Maybe your family is already destroyed because of what they did. I don't think you can blame Tom for any destruction. It's not like your family is in much better shape than mine."

"It's the past. They can't do anything other than apologize, and they've done that already. Multiple times."

No longer interested in showing Lance anything, she yanked her hand from his and glared straight ahead, biting her lower lip until they turned into her driveway. "I suppose you think I should forget about it too. Am I overreacting if I'm still upset?"

"I don't know what you want from them."

Determined to be honest, Kylie spoke softly. "I want them to suffer as much as I have because of what they did."

"It's not like they did it all by themselves."

"Of course not. I want them all to suffer. Your parents, my parents, and the staff at Middleton. Everyone who stole my son from me."

"What about the people who adopted Erick?"

"They loved him enough to adopt him. They're definitely not the problem."

Lance spoke softly as he turned off the Jeep. "You need to move on."

Narrowing her eyes, she shoved the door open to exit the truck. "Don't tell me what to do. Especially if it involves Erick. You get zero input unless I ask for your opinion." After slamming the door, she rushed up the sidewalk, unlocked the house, and went inside. By the time Lance came in, she'd changed out of her dress and into sweats and a T-shirt.

"I'm sorry," he said as he entered the bedroom. Instead of a heartfelt apology accompanied by a hug as she'd hoped for, all she got was an exasperated sigh as he stood in the doorway with a confused look on his face.

"Sure you are." Kylie brushed past him and went through the attic door. Instead of rushing up the stairs, though, she paused with her hand on the doorknob. After a few seconds of thought, she locked the door behind her. It was the first time she'd ever locked a door between her and Lance, but she was furious and didn't want to hear any more of his "advice" tonight.

Chapter 10

TOM PICKED UP his ringing cell phone and stared at the screen. "Eva," he muttered. "What does she want?" He took another swallow of Scotch before he answered the call.

"Merry Christmas, Tom! How's Minnesota?"

Her happy voice made him cringe. "Hey, Eva. How's Colorado?"

"It's all right. I wish you were here, though."

He chuckled at her lie. "Then why did you send me here instead?"

"Oh, stop. Let's not argue. I miss you."

He didn't want to mislead her, because he hadn't really missed her. He missed her as a friend and someone to laugh with on the couch or to drink with at the bar, but they hadn't done that since the accident. He'd been so upset by the combination of his inability to do anything on his own and knowing that Kylie had chosen Lance, that he just sat at home. "Is there any snow out there?"

"Yeah, the slopes are great. When are you going to be back in Montana?"

He finished his glass of Scotch to avoid answering right away. "I'm staying here."

"Right. For how long?"

"I'm not planning to come back to Montana, Eva. I'm going to stay here and try to straighten things out."

"Have you talked to your parents? How's it going?"

"Yeah, I went over there tonight. It's okay." Things had been okay until his mom told him about Lance and Kylie's upcoming wedding. Things weren't okay now. He'd acted like a complete asshole, and he didn't regret it for a second. Kylie's reaction to his dad referring to Erick as "your kid" instead of by name had made everything Tom said worthwhile.

He'd been stunned that Lance seemed dumbfounded that Kylie would be upset by not knowing where Erick was on

Christmas. What kind of person doesn't even consider a parent's feelings on such a family-oriented holiday?

"How are Lance and Kylie?"

Tom thought he heard a bit of a sneer in her voice as she said "Kylie," but chalked it up to his bad mood and the Scotch he'd drunk. "They're fine. I stayed with them for a couple of days before I decided to stay in Minnesota for good."

"How was that?"

There definitely was a whiny tone in her voice, which annoyed him. "It was fine. What did you think was going to happen if I came back here, Eva? You're the one who suggested that I come back and try to work with Kylie to find Erick."

"And have you found Erick?"

"Not yet. My investigator is working on it, though."

He heard a deep sigh through the phone.

"What's wrong, Eva?" He knew his voice was sharp, but he wanted the call to end.

"I miss you."

His foul mood from the entire night had worn away all of his patience. "We already covered that."

"You don't have to be such an asshole, though."

"I'm not being an asshole. You're the one who suggested this. So I can't really be blamed that you miss me. I'd have been perfectly happy to stay in Montana with you, or even without you." It was sort of the truth. He would have been just as happy in Montana as he'd been before he came home. It didn't really qualify as happy, though.

"What are you going to do when you find Erick?"

He poured another glass of Scotch. "Try to get custody of him."

"What about Kylie?"

He wanted her as much as he wanted Erick, but he wasn't cruel enough to voice it. "What about her?"

"Are you guys getting back together?" He could barely hear her voice.

"Mom told me tonight that Lance was going to propose to her." He was resigned. He'd had a chance to fix things with Kylie last summer, but he hadn't. She'd moved on to Lance, and Tom had to accept it and get on with his life.

"That doesn't answer my question."

"Really? You think I'd cock block my brother? You really do think I'm an asshole, don't you?" He wanted to fight. He wanted to drive her away so he didn't have to tell her it was over. He wanted everyone to leave him alone and let him wallow in his misery about missing out on his chance to be with Kylie again.

"I think you're obsessed with Kylie and Erick."

"I think you're forgetting that we're not serious." He glared at the window to the west of him, knowing she couldn't see him but still feeling as though he had to do something to show his displeasure.

"We've been living together."

Tom's eyes started to close. Finally, the Scotch had kicked in, and he didn't have to think anymore. "Night, Eva," he mumbled as he switched off the phone and dropped his head back on the couch.

Chapter 11

ON CHRISTMAS MORNING, Kylie woke in the attic when she heard a door slam outside. She turned her head toward the window and wiped the sleep from her eyes. Exhaust billowed from Lance's Jeep next to the garage. "Dammit," she muttered, rushing down the stairs. He couldn't leave. They were supposed to spend the day together. She didn't come to Chinkapin to spend Christmas alone.

She slid across the kitchen floor in her stocking feet and fought to open the door. "Lance, wait," she yelled as she yanked open the door and rushed out onto the porch. She ran directly into Lance's arms as he stepped back onto the porch.

He gripped her arms to steady her then backed away. "What's up?"

"I didn't want you to leave. I'm sorry." She gasped, suddenly realizing her knee hurt and reached down to rub it.

"What's wrong with your knee?"

"Nothing. I whacked it on the door frame as I rushed down from the attic. I thought you were leaving."

Lance steered her back into the house and shut the door. "I was starting my Jeep to let it warm up. I always go to my parents' house for breakfast on Christmas morning. I figured you wouldn't want to go with."

Kylie sat at the table and stared at him. She didn't want to go to his parents' house, but she didn't want to be alone, either. If she was going to be alone on Christmas Day, she might as well have stayed in Michigan. "When will you be back?"

Talking over his shoulder, he dug through the freezer. "I normally spend the whole day, but if you want, I'll come back right after breakfast, I suppose."

"Are you sure? I have a gift for you, but I don't want to ruin your plans." He hadn't even acknowledged her apology. Thinking he may not have heard her, she took a deep breath. "I'm sorry that I overreacted last night and ran away instead of dealing with our problems. I can't just forget what your parents and mine did."

"Yet you're willing to forgive yours and try to fix that relationship?"

"I'm trying, dammit, and I'm trying to not make this weird for you, but I'm angry, and you seem to think I should just forget about Erick."

"I never said that. I said that you should let go of the past and focus on the future. Our parents apologized."

She pressed her lips together and nodded. Their parents had apologized, just like he'd apologized last night. They said the words and expected everything to be okay without trying to understand her feelings.

"Don't you have an ice pack?"

"Probably not. It's fine." She stood and hobbled to the living room, where his gift sat next to the couch. "Do you want to open this now?"

"If you want to do it now, we can. Or we can do it when I get back."

She didn't want him to go. "How about now?"

He stood. "Let me go and get your present. It's in the closet."

"Or we could just open our presents in the bedroom. It's our Christmas. We can do whatever we want."

He crossed the room and lay his hand on top of the large silver-wrapped package she had for him. "Do you want me to carry this?"

"Sure."

A few moments later, they were sitting cross-legged on the bed, facing one another with presents in front of them. "You first," she said.

He took his time opening the box.

"Come on. It's just gift wrap. You can rip it."

He peeled off another piece of tape. "But this prolongs the excitement."

She wanted to see his reaction already. "Seriously, I'm going to open it for you if you don't hurry up."

"Am I supposed to guess what it is?"

"No, it'll take forever, and you'll never guess anyway."

"A drawing."

She laughed and leaned back on the pillows as she recalled the first time she apologized and gave him a drawing. They'd spent the day together on his couch, just being close to one another. He'd blown off his parents that day. "I'm not that predictable."

When he finally opened the box, he pulled out a pile of tissue paper then a smaller box. "Am I going to be opening boxes all day?"

"Doubtful."

He opened the smaller box and removed the watch. "Whoa. You bought me this? It's too expensive."

"No, it's not. You said you liked it, and I see you haven't bought it for yourself, so here you go."

He put the watch on and kissed her. "Thank you. It's great." He adjusted the time and set a small box in her lap.

"I'm glad you like it," she said as she tore the paper from her package. The whole time she was opening it, she hoped it wasn't an engagement ring. She wasn't ready to get married, and she definitely didn't want to ruin his Christmas by telling him so. "It's gorgeous," she exclaimed when she opened the jewelry box and found a gold necklace with a heart hanging from it.

"If you don't like it, we can return it. You're not an easy woman to shop for."

"No one is returning it. I love it." She put it on and rushed into the bathroom to look in the mirror. "It doesn't really go with this outfit," she called back to the bedroom as she quickly stripped down. Sex was a sure way to get him to stay.

"So change your clothes. You can come with me to my parents' for breakfast."

She froze with her panties around her knees then pulled them back up and yanked her T-shirt back on. All of her desire to hop in bed with him disappeared instantly. She didn't even want him around her anymore today. She pulled her scruffy sweatpants back on and returned to the bedroom. "I don't think so. I'll be here when you get back."

"Why don't you want to go with me?" He crossed the room, grasped her hips, and peered at her. "I thought everything was okay now."

She shook her head. "No, everything isn't okay. I'm not

going to your parents' house today, and I don't want to argue about it. You should go. When you come back, we can hang out together for the rest of the day."

"Or you could just come with me…"

"It's not going to happen." She walked out of the bedroom to start a fresh pot of coffee and make herself a bowl of oatmeal.

He walked up behind her and put his arms around her waist. "Mom makes French toast and crepes on Christmas morning," he whispered as he nuzzled the side of her neck.

"Dammit, Lance. I said I'm not going. Take a hint."

"Fine," he muttered. "Maybe Santa left you some Midol in your stocking."

She spun to face him. "Are you serious?"

He lifted his hands and backed away. "Just joking. I'll see you later."

Kylie watched him as he put on his jacket and boots, trying to figure out whether he seriously thought she had no reason to be upset.

* * *

Shortly after noon, Kylie was drinking her third cup of coffee in front of the fireplace and wondering just how long breakfast lasted at the Mallocks' house, when there was a knock at the door. She sighed and rose to her feet.

As she passed the kitchen window, she saw Tom's truck parked in the driveway. "Great," she muttered under her breath. Tom wasn't on her list of people she wanted to see or talk to, but then she remembered how miserable he'd looked the previous night. She pulled open the door.

He looked even worse today with his rumpled hair, unshaven face, and blurry eyes.

"Hey." She tried to ignore the memory of his fingers on her leg. "What's up?"

"I think we should talk."

She leaned against the door jamb and crossed her arms as she peered at him. "About what?"

His blue eyes met hers, and he sighed. "Erick."

She shivered and backed into the house, opening the door wide. "Come on in."

He stepped inside and removed his jacket, while Kylie turned away. "Coffee?" she asked over her shoulder. Instantly, her mind went back to their snowshoeing outing and how they'd almost kissed over the spilled coffee.

"Sure."

By the time she filled a blue mug and turned to hand it to him, he'd taken off his boots and stood next to the stove. He took the coffee. "Thanks. How's your hand?"

She held her hand up to show him it was fine. "I guess your quick thinking saved me from being scarred for life."

"I doubt I made that much difference."

She led him to the living room, where she settled on the couch and Tom sat in the recliner by the fireplace. "What do you want to talk about?"

"I want to find Erick."

Her heart raced, and she swallowed repeatedly. She still didn't think she could talk, though, so she nodded before gulping her coffee.

Tom leaned forward in the chair, resting his forearms on his knees. "I figured you'd have more to say about it than that."

Gazing into her cup, she thought of how badly she wanted to see Erick, to know what his life was like, to know he was okay, to tell him she'd wanted to keep him. Her voice was barely above a whisper. "Why? Don't you think I want to find him too?"

"If you wanted to find him, why haven't you been looking? You've known he's alive for months now."

"Four months." She looked down at her feet, and for some unknown reason, decided to tell him the truth. "I'm scared."

"Of what?"

"That he won't like me. That seeing him will break my heart." She took a deep breath, eyes on blurred lights twinkling in the boughs of the Christmas tree. "That his father will hurt him to hurt me."

"I wouldn't do that."

She picked up the bottle of Bailey's from the end table and dumped a healthy portion into her coffee. She capped it and set it back down without offering him any.

After pausing for a moment, he cleared his throat. "I've hired a private investigator to look for him. I'd appreciate it if you'd cooperate."

She swallowed and nodded. "I just want to make sure he's okay."

"He will be."

"I hope so."

"I mean once we find him, he'll be fine."

She cocked her head. "What do you mean by that?"

"I want custody."

"What?" Incredulous, she rose to stand directly in front of him, trying to ignore the memory of him pulling her onto his lap in the recliner. "Are you out of your mind? You can't do that."

"He's my son. I didn't agree to his adoption, and neither did you. We can get him back. Even if you don't want to be a part of my life, we can get joint custody of him."

"And destroy his life in the process? Someone wanted him badly enough to adopt him."

"You don't know what his life has been like."

"Neither do you. Besides, whoever adopted him loves him."

"How can you say that? How can you even start to imagine that some stranger loves our son more than we do?"

"I never said that." She ran her hands through her hair then twisted it into a knot. "He doesn't know us. Taking him from the family who has raised him would be like kidnapping him. How would you have liked it if some strangers showed up and took you away from your mom and dad?"

He grinned sardonically. "Depends on the day, I suppose."

"Didn't everyone feel that way about their parents as a teenager?" Kylie had, multiple times, even before her parents had sent her away.

After a moment, he touched her arm. "We can give him a better life than he's had."

"How do you know? You don't know anything about him or his family."

"We're his family."

"Biologically. But someone has loved him and raised him. They're his family."

"They have no right to be his family."

Kylie knew how Tom felt; she'd felt that way herself. She still felt that way sometimes, but she always convinced herself that it was better for her to suffer than to take Erick away from the family he knew and loved. She couldn't believe that Tom didn't have that same willingness to sacrifice his own happiness for Erick's. She rose from the couch and gestured toward the door. "You should leave."

"Why?"

Kylie crossed her arms. Maybe instead of just throwing him out because he didn't understand how she felt, she should explain it. "I don't want to ruin his life."

"I'm tired of my life being ruined."

She took a deep breath then sighed. She didn't know what kind of people had adopted him. It wasn't as though the people at Middleton had proven they were concerned about doing the right thing.

Tom cleared his throat. "It doesn't matter whether you help or not, or even if you want me to do it. I *will* find him."

"I know I can't stop you. I just don't think a custody fight is the answer. Maybe we can find him and be part of his life without ripping him away from the family he knows and loves. They love him. They love someone else's son, Tom—our son. That's pretty amazing, and we should respect and thank them for that. It's not like they're the ones who stole Erick. They're innocent in all of this too."

"You don't know that. They could be awful people. People who couldn't get approved to adopt anywhere else. Maybe they're just rich assholes like my parents, and they paid enough money to get what they wanted."

She could barely speak. "I have to believe they're good people. I'd die otherwise."

Tom walked toward the door. "I know how you feel, and you know how I feel. It's clear we don't agree. I'm going to find him, and I'm going to fight for custody."

Tom reached for the doorknob just as Lance strode in.

Lance paused for a fraction of a second with his foot in the air before recovering. "Tom, what are you doing here? Trying to *cajole* my girlfriend into doing something she doesn't want to do?"

"Just talking to Kylie about Erick."

Lance's gaze shifted from Tom to Kylie and back before settling on Kylie with drawn eyebrows. "How'd that go?"

"It went fine." Kylie crossed the room to Lance and kissed his cheek. "How was breakfast?"

"Good. I can't believe how much I've missed my parents." He narrowed his eyes at Kylie. "What's up with Erick?"

"Tom's going to find Erick." She took a deep breath. "Tom and I are going to find Erick." She wanted to find Erick to make sure he was okay. At least if she worked with Tom, she could try to change his mind about custody.

Lance arched an eyebrow. "Going to be one big happy family?"

Tom shook his head. "Not likely."

Annoyance bubbled up in Kylie, but she bit her lower lip to keep from screaming at Lance for his behavior. Nothing she had done with Tom indicated that she wanted to spend her life with him and Erick. Lance should have known her well enough to know that she would never break up Erick's current family. "Don't be ridiculous. Tom and I are friends, nothing more."

Tom turned his attention to Kylie and tipped his head to the side before grinning. "Yeah, absolutely nothing between us."

The silence pressed down on Kylie as she waited for Lance to respond.

After a moment, Tom cleared his throat. "On that note, I'm leaving. I'll keep you posted, Kylie."

"Sure." Once Tom had left the house, she turned to Lance. "What's with the attitude?"

After opening a beer and taking a swallow, he met her gaze with narrowed eyes. "The two of you are looking for Erick now?"

"He's my son. Don't I have a right to look for him?" She leaned against the kitchen counter, arms crossed and jaw clenched.

He took a deep breath. "Sure you do, but why with Tom?"

"Tom's his father. I can't stop him from looking." She heard the slight crinkle of the beer can as Lance tightened his grip.

Lance rummaged through the fruit bowl on the counter, selected an apple, and polished it on the front of his shirt. "Like you even want to stop him."

"What's that supposed to mean?" she asked as he took a big bite of the apple. His only response was to take another bite.

"He's your brother."

"You don't have to remind me."

"I'm not reminding you. I'm explaining myself, not that I should have to." She clenched her fists and fought to keep from shaking one at him. "What's the deal, Lance? Are you that insecure that I can't work with him to find our son?"

"I told you before that I don't trust him."

"What about me? You said you trusted me. Was that a lie? Are you going to tell the truth or press your lips together again like you do when you're lying?"

Lance finished the apple and tossed the core in the trash can. "I don't know what's going on with us. Since we came home, you've been different."

"Yeah? No kidding. It's Chinkapin. It's not like I can pretend the past didn't happen. We're all struggling to deal with it."

He turned to the sink to wash his hands. "I'm not."

"Of course not. It's not your past, Lance. It's mine and Tom's and our parents'. You just keep telling us all to get over it and let it go. Forgive and forget. It's not so easy for us."

She slammed her hands down on the counter. "If you can't deal with me dealing with my past, maybe you should leave. And if you can't deal with me being friends with Tom, you should definitely leave."

He closed the fridge, turned slowly, and gripped her arms. "Are you breaking up with me?"

She shook free of his grasp and moved to the other side of the kitchen. "I'm saying that you're acting like an asshole, and I'm not going to put up with it anymore. Either trust me and your brother and accept that we have stuff to work through, or leave me alone."

He moved toward her with his hands outstretched. "It's not that I don't trust you."

"It's that you're jealous of the time I spend with Tom. Right?" She backed away. "I think you should get your stuff and find somewhere else to stay."

"You don't even want to talk about it first?"

"We've talked about it multiple times. I don't like what you keep saying. Besides, you decided you were coming back to work here. You didn't even ask me if I wanted to stay in

Chinkapin. I thought we were going back to Michigan in February. If we keep talking, I'm going to like you even less than I do right now." She turned from him and rushed up to the attic, feet pounding on the wooden steps as she fought back tears.

She didn't want Lance to leave, but she didn't want him to keep acting as though he didn't trust her. Last summer, he hadn't seemed to have any issues with her being Tom's ex-girlfriend.

But now that she was on speaking terms with Tom, he was acting weird. She admitted that she was acting weird too, but she had all kinds of excuses as to why it was okay for her to act weird. Mainly, she just didn't want to deal with anyone.

Chapter 12

THE DAY AFTER Christmas, Tom sipped from his glass of Scotch and soda at the bar. He and Keefe had just finished a game of pool and were waiting for their burgers, when Vern Tallbaum slid onto the stool next to Keefe. "What's up, guys?"

"Nothing," Keefe replied.

"Mind if I join you?"

Tom shrugged. He didn't particularly like Vern because the guy had been a bully in elementary school. Tom assumed he'd grown out of that. He couldn't remember anything special about Vern from junior high or high school. "Doesn't bother me."

Keefe nodded. "Sure. What's new with you, Vern?"

"Nothing."

Tom tuned out their conversation as he thought about Kylie, Eva, and Erick. He kept going back to Kylie's expression when he'd left her in the Jeep with Lance. He couldn't really explain it, but he was certain she'd wanted to come in with him. Maybe she'd just wanted to escape Lance, but he doubted it. If she didn't still want him, why hadn't she moved away when he touched her leg. Instead, she'd covered his hand with her own.

It didn't mean anything, though. She was with Lance. Whether or not Tom wanted to be with her, it always came back to the fact that she was with Lance.

"I heard your cousin threw her boyfriend out."

Tom blinked and leaned forward to look past Keefe at Vern. "What?"

Keefe faced Vern. "Where did you hear that?"

"I overheard Mallock talking to someone at the grocery store."

Tom's shoulders relaxed. The only Mallock in town dating one of Keefe's cousins was Lance. He didn't know what had happened, but he intended to find out.

Just then, a woman with purplish black hair set his plate down in front of him with a *thunk*. "Need another drink?"

Scotch didn't seem so important anymore. "Nah. Thanks, though."

Keefe and Tom dug into their burgers, and Vern soon left since they were too busy eating to talk to him.

"What's with that guy?" Tom mumbled around a mouthful of French fries.

"Why?"

"I haven't seen him around since elementary school."

"He's been here. He'll never go anywhere else."

"Really? Why?"

Keefe shrugged. "No friends, no ambition, no life."

Tom shook his head. "I don't really care about him. What's this about Kylie throwing Lance out?"

"This is the first I've heard about it."

Tom rubbed his jaw as an idea started to form. He finished the last of his meal and wiped his mouth with a napkin. "What are you up to on New Year's Eve?"

"Probably sitting at Mira's. Why?"

"You guys should go out. We should go out. Bring Kylie with."

Keefe shook his head. "Nah. Mira doesn't like going out, especially on party nights. Too many people."

"Why not?"

"She had a bad experience. It's not my place to talk about it." He lifted his beer mug and took a swallow. "Besides, why do you want Kylie to come out?"

Tom grinned. "She threw Lance out. There must be a reason."

"So? He's your brother. Weren't you living with someone in Montana?"

"Why does everyone assume that Eva and I are madly in love?"

Keefe took a swallow of his beer and laughed. "You were living together. Everyone in this town knows that you never go out with the same woman more than four times. Of course we think it's serious if you've been living with someone."

Tom rubbed at the scar on his leg. He never went out with anyone more than four times because that's as long as it took before it became glaringly obvious that the women weren't anything like Kylie. The artist he'd dated had no morals. The redhead had no interest in being outside. The other redhead hated winter. "I'm not—wasn't—interested in anything serious."

"You think you and Kylie could be serious?"

Tom grinned. "We have a kid together."

Keefe leaned back and folded his arms across his chest. "What are you up to, Mallock?"

"I want her back. I love her. I've always loved her." He sighed. "I just haven't done anything about it because she's been with Lance. I wasn't about to destroy her relationship with him just to make myself happy, but…" He shrugged.

"But now that they're fighting, you're willing to go out with her?"

Tom didn't want to seem that opportunistic, and he didn't want to talk about Kylie's touch, or their near kiss. "I want to see if there's a chance for us. If you guys invite her out on New Year's Eve, I can find out if she's still interested in me."

"If she was interested in you, why didn't she start dating you last summer instead of Lance? Why didn't you tell her you were interested before she got together with Lance?"

Tom had asked himself the same question many times but never came up with an appropriate response. "Because I was mad at her."

"You mean you thought she chose to get rid of him?"

Ashamed of his reaction to Kylie's return to Chinkapin last summer, Tom gazed at his empty glass and nodded. "Yeah, I was an asshole. I'm trying to fix it now."

"Why don't you just ask her out? Leave me and Mira out of it?"

Tom chuckled. "I don't have that much faith in my abilities. I doubt she'd go out with me, but if we both happened to show up at the same place, I might have a chance."

"What if she's not really over Lance? What if they're just arguing? You could ruin any chance of them getting back together. You're willing to do that to your brother?"

"It's not like I'm going to force her into anything. You know me better than that, Keefe. I just want a chance. If she's not interested, she's not interested. If she is interested, she is."

"Then why not just ask her out yourself?"

"Because…" He sighed. "I'm afraid she'll say no."

"So you want me to convince Mira to go out—which she hates—and to have her lie to her best friend so Kylie will show up at the bar while you're here on New Year's Eve?"

"Yeah, pretty much." Tom flashed a smile at Keefe. "I did agree to be your best man. Help a friend out?"

Chapter 13

THE NEXT EVENING, Kylie saw the headlights coming down the driveway and hoped it wasn't Lance coming back to force her to work things out. When Mira's tiny red hatchback parked beneath the security light in front of the garage, Kylie frowned and set down her pencil and sketch pad.

She went downstairs to wash her hands, moving slowly. She knew she should just call Lance and apologize, but she also thought he'd accepted her directive pretty willingly. Maybe he was tired of being with her. Maybe he'd just been waiting for a chance to leave. Or maybe he was right. Maybe she hadn't hidden her feelings for Tom as well as she'd thought.

After letting herself in, Mira removed her boots and coat. She'd barely entered the kitchen before hugging Kylie. "What's going on with you?"

Kylie froze at the sink and wiped her hands on a yellow dish towel as she faced Mira. "What do you mean?"

"Keefe told me that everyone's fighting."

"Everyone?"

"Well, you, Tom, and Lance."

"I'm not fighting with Tom, at least not any more than I was last summer. Maybe even less. Besides, Lance and I aren't fighting. We're just not speaking."

"You threw him out."

"How do you know this already? It's been less than a day."

"Someone said something about it at the bar when Tom and Keefe were playing pool last night. Keefe saw Lance at the grocery store this morning. Lance told him he's staying at his mom and dad's."

Kylie opened the fridge and took out a bottle of wine. "I didn't throw him out. I suggested he leave if he didn't want me to deal with my past."

"What's that mean?" Mira retrieved two wine glasses from the cabinet and held them while Kylie poured.

"He's paranoid that something's going on between Tom and I."

"Is there?"

"Are you out of your ever-loving mind?"

"Probably." Mira smiled. "I am marrying your cousin."

"Good point." Kylie carried the bottle over to the table and sat. While sipping her wine, she wondered if maybe talking to Mira would make things clearer to her. "Tom wants to find Erick. I want to find Erick. It makes sense for the two of us to do it together."

Mira raised an eyebrow. "That's it?"

"Yes. That's it. Lance should know I'm not interested in Tom." Kylie couldn't meet Mira's gaze.

"You have been spending more time with Tom."

"No shit." She frowned. "Any time with him is more time than I've spent with him since I left eleven years ago. Besides, the only time I've spent alone with him was when we went snowshoeing and once to talk about finding Erick."

"Anything exciting happen?"

Kylie stared at the table and sighed. "I almost kissed him when we went snowshoeing."

Mira let out a little squeal. "What? I want details."

Kylie waved her hand in a dismissive motion. "I don't really want to talk about Tom, okay?"

Mira took a long swallow of wine then nodded reluctantly. "You're going to have to tell me sometime."

"What's going on with the wedding plans?"

"Not much. We're still on for Valentine's Day."

Kylie scrunched her nose up but sipped her wine. Just because she thought getting married on Valentine's Day was ridiculous didn't mean she was going to tell Mira that.

"I know it's cheesy, and I don't particularly care. Keefe agreed, so that's all that counts."

"Fair enough." Kylie refilled her wine glass. "Will we all be dressing up as valentines, then?"

"Why? Do you want to wear red and pink with lots of lace?"

"Um…" Kylie shook her head. "I think I'll leave that for my own special occasions. In private."

Mira snorted. "Good thing I wasn't drinking, or I would

have had wine coming out my nose. I decided on sheath dresses in dove gray. Pink tulips. Simple and elegant."

"Wow. That sounds pretty awesome. I figured you'd do something a bit more traditional." Kylie had always imagined she would be married in a traditional wedding, surrounded by friends and family. Except now, her friends and family wouldn't fill the first two rows of the Lutheran church she'd attended as a little girl.

"Because I'm so traditional and predictable?"

Kylie shrugged. "Well, yeah. Not that it's bad to be traditional."

"But predictable is boring."

"Is it?" Kylie stretched her feet out, propped them on the chair opposite her, and pushed the hair out of her face. "I could go for some traditional predictability right about now. I'm getting tired of all the surprises the Mallocks are throwing at me."

"You could cut bait and run. Or should I say you can head back to Michigan since you already broke up with Lance?"

"I've thought about it, but if I was going to do that, I shouldn't have come back from Michigan. Should I?" Before Mira could answer, she continued. "Besides, I want to find Erick. Tom wants to find Erick. Maybe if we're both here, both working at it, we'll find him."

"Well, you're stuck here until after my wedding, anyway. After that, if you want to leave, I'll understand." She held up her hand before Kylie could speak. "I'll miss you like crazy of course, but I'll understand."

"And you'll have your new husband to entertain and comfort you."

"Exactly. Is there something wrong with that?"

"Nope. I'm so happy for both of you. It's about damn time." Jealousy twinged in Kylie's stomach. She really was happy for both of them; she just wished that she was as certain about the future as her cousin and best friend were.

"Yeah. Too bad it took so long for me to get to this point, huh?"

"Everything works out the way it's supposed to. At least that's what I keep telling myself."

Mira stared toward the window, twisting her finger in her

hair. "I hope you're right."

"What do you mean?"

"I'm…" She frowned then turned to Kylie. "I hope everything works out with Keefe and I."

"Why wouldn't it?"

"On our wedding night, you know?"

Kylie tilted her head and swallowed a couple of times before replying. "You mean you and Keefe haven't…"

"Yeah. I've never. Well, not since that night when we were in junior high. I hope I don't freak out on him."

Kylie searched her brain, trying to find the right words. Once she realized that nothing she could say would erase the past or set Mira's mind at ease, she just told her friend what she felt. "Keefe knows you were raped. I'm sure he'll understand if you need to take it slow or even stop. He loves you."

Mira wiped at her eyes. "I know. Still, I worry about it. I don't want to cry about this. That asshole shouldn't have the power to make me cry still. It's been ages. I should be over it."

Kylie rose and hugged Mira. "I know, sweetie, but the thing is, everyone heals at different rates. You'll be fine. You *are* fine. Whatever you feel right now is what you're supposed to feel."

Mira shook her head, moving her hair out of her face. "Enough worrying about that. What are you up to on New Year's Eve?"

"Sitting home alone."

"You don't think you're going to work things out with Lance before then?"

"I doubt it. He just walked out when I told him to. He didn't even argue about it."

Mira's gentle chuckle filled the room. "Like you gave him a chance to argue about it. I bet you shouted out your demand then turned and ran for your attic fortress."

"It's not a fortress. It's my sanctuary."

"Yes, yours. No one dares go up there without your welcome."

Kylie returned to her chair. Maybe Mira was right; maybe Lance had left just because she'd ordered it, not because he wanted to.

"You should come out with us on New Year's Eve."

"And be a third wheel? I don't think so."

"Come on. It'll be fun."

Kylie couldn't think of anything fun about going out in Chinkapin on New Year's Eve.

"Keefe really wants to go out, but I…"

Kylie reached over to pat Mira's hand, knowing how much her friend dreaded being around people she wasn't close to, especially when there was drinking. Kylie's presence would make it easier on Mira, even though Keefe would be there too. "I'll go. Just for you."

Mira's smile lit up her face. "Thanks. You're the best."

"Yeah. Right."

"Tom is going to meet us at the bar."

Kylie closed her eyes and took a deep breath. When she opened her eyes, she nodded once. "Is that why you came over here? Just to convince me to go on a double date with Tom and you two?"

Mira grinned. "Do you want to go on a date with Tom?"

After draining her wine glass, Kylie shrugged. "What the hell? It's not like Lance and I are together anymore, right?"

Chapter 14

TOM WAS AT the bar when Kylie entered on New Year's Eve. He paused with his glass of whiskey halfway to his mouth as he watched her make her way across the room to join Mira and Keefe. When she removed her long down parka, he gulped his drink. He'd never seen her dressed like she was tonight. Instead of her normal jeans and sneakers, she wore a sleeveless knee-length black dress. It wasn't revealing, but it hugged her slender body in all the right places, causing his hands to twitch with the urge to trace her curves.

He turned sideways, resting his elbow on the bar, while he kept his gaze on her. Even though he'd asked Keefe to convince her to come, he hadn't expected her to show up. He just didn't think he was that lucky.

"She's something, huh?"

Tom turned his attention to the man next to him. It was Vern Tallbaum. "What?"

"That Killian chick. Flouncing around like she's something special. Couldn't even show up for her own sister's funeral. She's always thought she was better than the rest of this town."

Tom inclined his head a fraction of an inch, almost wishing he'd been sitting there longer. If he'd had a few drinks, he would have been willing to beat the piss out of the guy for saying something like that about Kylie. Instead, he was sober and didn't intend to get into a bar fight. At least not tonight. Tonight, his goal was to convince Kylie to give him a second chance. She wasn't marrying Lance—at least not right now—and that gave him a chance. He wasn't going to blow that chance by getting into a fight.

"I never noticed that about her."

"Here you go," the bartender said, setting a glass next to Tom.

"Thanks." Tom slid a twenty across the bar. "Keep the change." He knew the bartenders put up with a lot of crap from him when he was drunk. So when he wasn't drunk, he always tipped well.

The bartender grinned. "She's a bitch."

Tom held the bartender's gaze for a few seconds, trying to place him. "Scott Killian, right?" Kylie's brother used to work at the plant owned by the Mallocks, but his hair was longer now, and he'd grown a scraggly beard.

Scott nodded. "And you're Tom Mallock. What's your point?"

"I thought you worked at the plant. At least you used to. What happened?"

Scott wiped the counter, scowling at Tom. "What does it matter to you?"

Tom didn't really care, but Scott had been one of his employees. He'd been a fairly good worker, as far as Tom knew. "Just curious why you decided to leave? Mallock Manufacturing tries to treat their employees well."

"Yeah, well, your dad has different ideas on how to treat the help." He crumpled the bar rag and shrugged nonchalantly. "I got busted on a drug charge. When I was done serving my time, my job was gone."

Tom nodded. "That happens. Besides, our asses are on the line if someone gets hurt at the plant because of drug use. We can't risk the safety of our crews."

"Yeah. That's the BS story he gave me too. I suspect he was thrilled to get rid of a Killian. Too bad he can't get rid of Kylie, huh?"

"Why would he want to get rid of Kylie?" Tom forced his fist to relax and tapped his fingers on the bar, wishing for a subject change.

Vern laughed. "Come on, Mallock. You're not that clueless, are you? It's all over town that Kylie got knocked up with a Mallock baby. No one knows whether it was yours or your brother's."

Tom raised his chin. "Really?" He finished his drink. "I didn't know the world cared that much about the Mallocks."

"So whose was it?" Vern asked.

Tom wondered if he could play dumb enough to convince Tallbaum he had no idea what he was talking about. "What baby are you talking about? I've never seen Kylie with a baby."

"Of course not," Scott said. "She ran off and had an abortion. Then she blackmailed your parents into paying for her to go to that stupid art school in Michigan."

Tom blinked. From what Kylie had told him when they were younger, she had doted on her younger brother and sister. He'd always assumed that Scott Killian felt the same love toward Kylie. "You're saying shit like that about her? She's your sister, for God's sake."

"Nah. We just have the same parents. She doesn't mean a fucking thing to me. If she was my sister, she would have been here for Kristy's funeral."

Tom heard a gasp and looked over to see Kylie standing a few feet from the bar. Before he could approach her, she spun away and headed back toward the table. He assumed she was about to grab her coat and leave. He slammed his hand on the bar. "Your other sister? You really think Kylie chose not to be here for that? I guess I can see why Kylie hates this town."

"I just don't know why you're defending her after all she's done to your family."

Tom narrowed his eyes. "Someone sure as hell has to defend her if even her own brother is spreading lies."

Chapter 15

KYLIE RETURNED TO the table and grabbed her coat. "I'm sorry, Mira. I can't do this."

Mira's forced smile made her look as though she was at a public execution instead of a bar on New Year's Eve. "Why? What happened?"

"Tom's up at the bar chitchatting with my brother and Vern Tallbaum. They seem pretty friendly."

Mira's nose wrinkled. "Vern's here?"

"Of course he's here. He's always here."

"But what—"

Before Mira could voice her concern, Kylie nodded. "I know. You'll be fine. Keefe won't leave you alone."

Keefe touched Mira's hand. "We can go if you want."

Mira forced a smile and shook her head. "No. I know how much you wanted to come out tonight. We'll just stay away from him. It'll be fine."

Proud of Mira's unwillingness to run away from her rapist, Kylie wished she had some of Mira's backbone. "I just can't deal with Tom sitting there, listening to their lies about me."

She slid her arms into her coat and turned from the table toward the door. Then she froze. Tom stood next to the door. His faded jeans and T-shirt could have been the same ones he'd worn in high school. He looked unchanged to her tonight, and when he grinned, her stomach twisted and flipped just as it had when she was fifteen.

"Going somewhere?" he asked when she stopped in front of him.

"Yeah. Home."

"Why?"

She glanced toward the bar. "Look, Tom. I heard you guys."

"You should have stuck around to hear more, then."

Kylie pursed her lips and shook her head. "You don't want me here any more than I want to be here. Let's just leave it at that."

"You're wrong. I'm the reason Mira asked you to come out tonight. I want to be here with you very much."

Kylie stepped back in shock.

"You look great," he said.

"Thanks. You too." She hadn't even drunk anything, and she'd returned a compliment. If this was a sign of how the night was going to go, it might be prudent for her to turn tail and run back to her attic.

He cocked his head and raised his eyebrows.

"Never mind. Just being polite." She wasn't ready to admit to him that she was still attracted to him.

He shifted closer, and his breath caressed the side of her face. "No, you weren't."

Leaning away, she hoped her face was still as pale as ever and not as red as it felt. "Are you saying I'm not polite?"

"Not to me. We're closer than that."

"Closer than polite?"

"Closer than lying to be polite." He touched the back of her hand then loosely circled her wrist with his fingers. "Aren't we?"

Kylie trembled at his touch then met his gaze and nodded. "I guess we probably are past that point."

"Exactly." He gestured toward the bar. "What can I get you to drink?"

"Beer."

"Really? Just beer? What kind?"

Her arm was on fire from his touch, and her heart pounded. "Surprise me."

"Is this some sort of test?"

"Really? How hard can it be? You drank beer at my house. You bought beer to replace the beer you drank." She'd convinced herself it was okay to see Tom tonight, even okay to flirt with him. Lance didn't trust her, and they weren't together. Tugging her arm free, she nodded toward Mira and Keefe's table. "I'll be over there."

He flashed the smile that Kylie had fallen in love with when she was fifteen. "I'll be right there."

She fought the urge to fan herself with her hand as she made her way back to Mira and Keefe's table.

"What was that?" Mira asked as Kylie slid into her chair.

"I'm not sure." Tom had always been able to arouse Kylie, but tonight, it was as if he just had to look at her to make her stomach clench in anticipation of his touch.

"Do I even want to know what the two of you were talking about?" Keefe asked with a baffled look.

"Probably not." Mira patted his cheek. "Why don't you go get us some drinks?"

"I don't need another drink," Keefe said.

"Just go do something, then. I want to talk to Kylie."

Keefe stood. "Your wish is my command, my soon-to-be bride."

"Excellent." Mira smiled up at him, and for the first time since Kylie had arrived, her best friend looked as though she was enjoying herself.

"Need anything?" Keefe asked Kylie.

"No, I'm good. Tom's getting me a beer."

When Keefe left the table, Mira leaned closer to Kylie. "Are you and Tom…?"

"I don't know what I'm doing. I just…" Kylie ran her hands over her hair. "I'm curious, I guess. Was it just a teenage thing? Or, you know, could it be like what you and Keefe have?"

"What about Lance?"

Kylie's heart sank. She knew she shouldn't be thinking about Tom, but it was impossible not to think about him in that way when he looked at her as if she were the most desirable woman in the world. "I know. Lance is great. Other than his inability to get over the past." She stretched her leg out and nudged Mira with her foot. "Shush. Here comes Tom."

Mira picked up her nearly empty glass. "Should I leave you alone?"

"No."

"Not ever, or not now?"

"Not now. Maybe later."

"Maybe later, what?" Tom asked as he stopped behind Kylie's chair and reached over her to set her beer on the table.

His scent surrounded her, and she could feel the warmth of him right behind her. She smiled over her shoulder at him as she resisted the urge to lean back against him. "Maybe later, I'll tell Mira what I think of her bridesmaid dresses. I haven't seen them yet, but I'm doubtful that I'll like them. Mira's more floral than I am."

"I promise the dresses are not floral print."

"What about the tuxes?" Tom asked.

"Just yours." Mira grinned at him. "You're the best man. Of course your tux will be special."

Kylie noticed that Tom was drinking from a can of Coke. "What's up?" she asked, pointing at it.

"I'm not drinking tonight."

"Why?" Her heart stopped as she worried. If Tom was drunk, it wouldn't matter so much if she flirted with him, but if he was sober, he would know exactly what was going on. He would remember tomorrow if she made a fool of herself.

He smiled that smile again. "I figured I'd be the designated driver. Isn't it my turn?"

"For who?"

He trailed a finger from her elbow to her wrist. "You?"

Kylie swallowed, wondering if he had the same questions as her about their past and present relationships. "We'll see about that." She wanted to see about lots of things, but she wasn't about to give herself permission to find out if his kisses still twisted her into knots.

"At least you didn't shoot me down right away."

"That's true."

Keefe returned to the table and leaned close to whisper to Mira before she stood and followed him out onto the dance floor. Kylie watched them, chin in hand, elbow propped on the table.

"What are you thinking?" Tom asked, scooting a chair close to hers so they could hear one another over the music.

"They're so perfect for each other. I'm glad they're together. Finally."

From the corner of her eye, she saw him nod. "They're good for each other. Lucky for them."

Unsure of how to proceed, Kylie shifted in her chair and faced Tom. "What is it you want from me?" She wasn't sure how she wanted him to answer. Part of her wanted him to say, "nothing," while another part of her wanted him to say, "everything."

He acted as though he'd been waiting for her to ask. He didn't seem surprised and didn't pause before answering. "Another chance."

"Don't you think we should just let the past stay in the past?" She raised a hand when he started to speak. "I'm not even talking about Erick right now. I'm just talking about you and I."

"Don't you wonder what it would be like?"

"Maybe sometimes, but that doesn't mean we should do anything about it. It doesn't mean we should or shouldn't be together. Or that we should try recapturing our youth." She'd imagined them together, but it was more of a memory of how they used to be. She couldn't picture herself staying in Chinkapin to date him, and she couldn't picture him in her apartment in Michigan. The only image she had of them together as adults was lying next to him naked on the braided rug in front of the fireplace at her grandparents' house, covered with the quilt from the couch. She gulped her beer.

"True." Tom took a swallow of his soda. When he set it down, he took her hand in his. The coolness of his skin surprised her, but when he rubbed his thumb over the back of her hand, she forced herself to freeze instead of relaxing into his grasp.

"If you're not even a little bit interested, why can I see your pulse jumping?"

"You can't. You're imagining things."

"No, I'm not." He leaned closer and pressed his lips to her throat.

Kylie's eyes fluttered shut, and she gasped. She could feel the heat from his mouth all the way down to her toes as she tipped her head to the side.

"Right there," he whispered as he pulled back.

The loss of his touch chilled her enough to cause a shiver.

"Want to dance?" he asked, still caressing her hand with his thumb.

"I…" She cleared her throat and tried again. "I suppose we can do that."

"You suppose?" He winked. "Either you want to or you don't. Your choice."

Kylie couldn't bring herself to say she wanted him to kiss her more, so instead, she nodded and stood, forcing herself to ignore the eyes she felt on her. Ninety percent of the people in town already hated her. Dancing with her ex-boyfriend's brother wasn't going to change that. "Let's dance."

"I thought you'd never ask." Tom rose from his chair and led her to the edge of the dance floor. He took her in his arms, and she rested her palms on his shoulders.

She held herself away from him, but the heat from his hand on her waist seeped into her, almost as though it was trying to melt her resolve.

When the music stopped, she stepped back, sliding her hands down his chest. Instead of letting go, he pulled her closer, tipped her head up with a finger under her chin, and lowered his mouth to hers. He kissed her gently with barely any pressure to it, just the lightest of touch.

His mouth felt like coming home. Pressing against him, she looped her hands around his neck, wanting more. She opened her mouth and touched his lips with her tongue.

With a growl, he slid a hand up from her hip to the back of her head, adjusting the angle to deepen the kiss. After a few seconds, Tom gentled the kiss and moved back a little.

She glanced around the room and froze when she saw Scott watching her. He curled his lip in a sneer and turned away. "Excuse me," she whispered and jerked free of Tom's embrace.

"Why?"

Mira smiled at her from across the room, and Kylie's eyes burned. Too many people were watching her. "I need to use the restroom."

Tom guided her toward the hallway that led to the restrooms. "Or are you trying to run away from me?"

"No." Kylie tried to sound normal, even though she felt as if the world had started spinning backward. "I just need a little space to straighten out my thoughts."

"I don't want your thoughts straightened out if it means you won't kiss me again."

Kylie caught her lower lip between her teeth. "I can't do this here. I don't know if I can do this at all, but definitely not here. Not in front of everyone."

Tom trailed his hand up and down her bare arm. "Do

what?"

Kylie swallowed, trying to find her resolve. "I'm not sure. Maybe I want to know what we could have."

"You do?"

"Yeah, but I don't want to hurt Lance. I don't want to hurt anyone."

"I know he's my brother and you care about him, but are you serious? How much does he really care about you? He didn't stand up for you on Christmas Eve. I bet he thinks you should just get over the past."

Kylie looked away, hoping to hide how accurate his statements were.

Tom's hand paused on hers then wrapped around it. "He didn't tell you he wanted to stay in Chinkapin, and he doesn't know how you feel about Erick being gone."

"You and I getting together—if we do—doesn't change my mind about finding Erick."

"Not even a little?"

She shook her head and narrowed her eyes. "I'm serious, Tom. Erick isn't part of our do-over. Leave him out of it and don't bug me about changing my mind about seeking custody."

He leaned closer, turned her hand over, and traced a heart on her palm. "Or what?"

"Or I'm done even considering giving you another chance."

"Even though you just kissed me like you wanted to tear my clothes off?"

Kylie's face felt hot, but she wasn't going to deny how she'd reacted. "Yeah, even though I kissed you like I wanted to tear your clothes off."

He edged closer, touching her arm. "But as long as I don't mention him, you'll consider kissing me again."

Kylie fought to keep her breathing even. When she had decided to come out tonight with Mira and Keefe, she'd known she would see Tom. She'd even decided to try getting to know him again, but her traitorous body was ready to jump into bed with him. "Maybe," she said with a smile.

He pressed his lips to the corner of her mouth. "Good." He stepped back. "Need another drink?"

"Sure. One more. This time, make it a rum and Coke."

Tom raised an eyebrow. Kylie turned on her heel and went

into the restroom. She didn't need the facilities; she needed to get away from Tom long enough to calm her frazzled nerves.

Chapter 16

TOM MADE HIS way back to the bar and ordered Kylie's drink and a Coke for himself. Once he had the beverages, he took them to the table and sat with Keefe and Mira. "Having a good time?" he asked.

Mira shrugged. "It's not as bad as I expected, but…"

"But you'd rather not be here?" Keefe asked.

She nodded. "I'm okay. I'm glad to help you out, Tom."

"Why? Do you know something I don't?"

"Of course I know things you don't. Women always know more about some things than men do."

"Like what?" Tom grinned, hoping Mira would tell him something he didn't know about Kylie's feelings toward him. But what could she tell him other than Kylie was still interested, or at least attracted to him? He'd picked up on that all by himself already.

Mira's laugh rang loud and clear over the ruckus of the bar. "I'm not telling you any of Kylie's secrets if that's what you're getting at."

He leaned closer. "What kind of secrets?"

Mira's gaze shifted over Tom's shoulder, and her smile faded as she shook her head. "I was just teasing. I don't know Kylie's secrets. Remember? You were one of her secrets. She's really good at keeping them."

Tom glanced behind him, hoping to see Kylie, but she wasn't there. When he faced Mira again, she gestured toward the restrooms. "You're not here to visit with me or Keefe. Go find Kylie."

"Why? She can find her way back to the table by herself, can't she?"

Keefe frowned slightly and tipped his head toward the hallway Kylie had gone down.

Tom wasn't sure why Keefe was trying to get rid of him, but he stood. "You're right. I didn't come here to visit with you guys."

As Tom made his way down the hall, he heard scuffling noises and an angry voice. "Leave me alone, asshole."

His stride quickened, and he pushed open the door that said "Employees Only." "Everything okay in here?"

The purplish-haired waitress who'd served him earlier smiled at him in relief. "Everything's fine." She tugged the bottom of her shirt to straighten it and blinked rapidly.

Tom met the man's gaze who stood a few feet away from the waitress. "Tallbaum? What's going on?"

"None of your damn business, Mallock." Vern glared at the waitress, pushed past Tom, and returned to the bar.

"Are you okay?" Tom asked.

"I'm fine. He just thinks…" She wiped at her face and looked away. "He seems to think I've been flirting with him because I serve him drinks."

"Did he hurt you?"

"No. Thank you for barging in." She picked up a cardboard box. "I have to get back to work."

"Can I carry that for you?"

"It's napkins. Not heavy, and it's my job." Her voice shook.

"Cool." He backed out of the room.

Her voice was gentler. "Thank you again. Drinks are on me tonight."

He laughed. "I'm not drinking, but thanks for the offer."

As the waitress shut and locked the supply room, the door of the women's restroom opened, and out walked Kylie. Tom took a moment to appreciate her curves as he followed her down the hallway. Just before she stepped out onto the dance floor, he dropped his hand on her shoulder.

She spun around, bringing her hands up in a boxing position. "What the fuck do you think you're doing?" she snarled.

Tom lifted his hands and took a step back. "Whoa, Kylie. What's the problem?"

She quickly dropped her hands, and her glower faded. "Oh. It's you."

He stepped closer, unsure of whether or not he should touch her. "Are you okay?"

She swallowed a couple of times then nodded. "Sorry. I

didn't know you were there, and you startled me."

"I didn't mean to." When he'd startled people before, they would flinch or jump a little, not spin around with murder in their eyes. "I didn't know you were so jumpy."

She forced her lips to curl into a smile. "I'm just a little out of sorts. How about that drink?"

He nodded. "Yeah. I left it at the table with Mira and Keefe."

"Perfect. Thanks." She spun away and quickly wove her way through the crowd to the table, where she sat down and drank half of her rum and Coke without another word.

Chapter 17

THE REST OF the evening was lighthearted, but sexually charged. Kylie and Tom danced a few more times, but the dances never ended in another kiss. Kylie didn't know whether she was happy about that or disappointed. Tom touched her hand, her arm, and her back at random times while they talked with their friends at the table, but it wasn't sexual—unless she considered how aware of his presence his touches made her.

She couldn't figure out why he'd backed off, but she was grateful. She didn't want to make a fool of herself tonight. She didn't want the entire bar to know how she felt about Tom. Because if the bar knew, then the town would know, and if the town knew, then Lance would know. The last thing she wanted to do was hurt Lance.

When the clock struck midnight, Tom took Kylie in his arms and kissed her. Kylie had been anticipating and dreading that moment since he'd walked up to the table with her drink after their first dance. The kiss was… nice. Tom gave her a bit more than a simple peck. It wasn't as deep or passionate as the one on the dance floor, and Kylie didn't want to crawl inside him to be closer, but she wanted more from the kiss. She wanted more from Tom.

She finished the drink that was in front of her. It was her third rum and Coke, and she was pleasantly buzzed. Mira and Keefe were occupied with one another, and Tom was chatting with someone over by the pool table.

She stood and was buttoning her jacket, when someone bumped into her from behind. When she turned, she saw Vern Tallbaum. He'd been a couple of years ahead of her in high school and a jerk then.

"Excuse me," she said.

"There's no excuse for someone like you." Vernon glared at her. "Why'd you come back to Chinkapin? No one wants you here." He was slurring so much, Kylie could barely understand him.

"Okay. Whatever you say." Kylie backed away. Even though what he said may have been true for the majority of Chinkapin's population, she didn't really care what they thought of her anymore. Besides, she knew Vern was drunk.

Tom appeared by her side. "Ready to go, Kylie?"

She nodded. "Yeah, but I'm fine. You can stay if you want." She hoped he wouldn't let her leave alone, but she didn't want to make him feel obligated.

"I don't want to stay. I want to drive you home." He took her hand in his and smiled coldly at Vernon. "Anything else, Vern?"

Vern curled his lip and shook his head. "No."

Tom and Kylie said their goodbyes to their friends, and Mira hugged Kylie. While Kylie hugged her back, Mira spoke in her ear. "Are you sure this is what you want to do? You have to choose one of them. You can't string them both along."

Kylie backed away, refusing to meet her best friend's gaze. She knew she couldn't have both of them, and she resented Mira for acting as though Kylie was expecting to have a relationship with both Lance and Tom. Her blood was boiling when they stepped outside. Thankfully, it wasn't as cold as normal on New Year's. This year, it was around twenty degrees, but she felt warm.

When Tom's thumb caressed the back of her hand, she shifted a little closer to him. Tom had always been great at calming her and arousing her.

He tugged her close enough to drape his arm around her shoulders. She watched her boots as they walked across the dimly lit parking lot. Slush and ice topped her toes. She glanced up at him and was amazed to see his gaze. His eyes were intent on her, and he didn't appear to have any other interests in the world.

"What are we doing, Tom?" she whispered when they stopped next to his truck.

Instead of removing his arm so she could get in the truck, he pulled her around so they were face-to-face. "I missed you. I missed kissing you and talking to you." He brushed his lips over hers. "I missed loving you."

Kylie tried to ignore the flutter she felt in her chest as his fingers twined through her hair. Instead, she leaned into the kiss and parted her lips. His tongue swept into her mouth, touching hers, and she gasped. Her knees wobbled, and she slid her hands up to his chest, needing his support and needing to feel his heart racing like hers. She didn't remember his kisses being like this. No longer did he seem unsure of himself. He acted as if he knew exactly the way to weaken her knees along with her resolve.

The small portion of her brain that was able to think tried to pull away from him. Instead, she drew him closer, and he backed her up against the door of his truck. Needing to feel his skin beneath her fingers, she slipped her glove off and ran her fingers up to his neck.

Suddenly, he stepped back, lifting his hands from her. Dazed, Kylie stared at him before realizing they were lit up by the headlights of a vehicle. She turned toward the vehicle and recognized the front of a Jeep Wrangler. "Fuck," she muttered and ran her hands through her hair as she turned away. The last person she needed witnessing her loss of sense was Lance.

Not that it mattered who saw it. In Chinkapin, gossip flew faster than any bird.

"Fuck him. You're not dating anymore. You can kiss anyone you want." Tom tried to pull her back into his embrace, but she spun away to rush to the Jeep.

"Lance, wait. It's not what it looks like." She yanked open the door and put her hand on his where it rested on the steering wheel. His eyes narrowed as he clenched his jaw and swallowed.

"Are you sure? Because it looked like you were kissing my brother." His voice was cold and emotionless.

Eager to defend herself, she shook her head. Even after drinking too much, she couldn't—she wouldn't—lie to him. "Fine. I was kissing him, but it doesn't mean anything. I had too much to drink. I was lonely." She squeezed his hand as her eyes burned. "It was a mistake."

"If you miss me, you have a weird way of showing it. Besides, you're the one who told me to move out."

"Only because you refused to trust me."

He arched an eyebrow in the green glow of the instrument panel. "For good reason, obviously."

Stepping up next to Kylie, Tom placed a hand on her shoulder. "Like you've never made a mistake, Lance?"

"Clearly, I have. Take tonight for example. I came here, looking for the woman I love, thinking she might be interested in working out our differences after I apologized for not believing she didn't have feelings for her ex anymore. Definitely a mistake."

Kylie shrugged out from under Tom's arm. Instead of being stubborn this time, she was willing to beg. "Don't do this, Lance. Please, let me explain."

"No." Lance shook her hand from his and reached for the handle to pull his door shut.

She was still pleading with him when he slammed the door and drove away. She turned to Tom. "I want to go home."

"Okay." He led her to his truck and opened the passenger door.

She got in and buckled her seat belt as he rounded the front of the truck. When he didn't say anything as he started the truck, she reached out and touched his hand.

He pulled away from her. "I'll take you home."

"What's wrong?"

"Us being together, obviously. I'm a mistake."

Kylie hit her leg with a fist and swore. "You're not a mistake, dammit."

"You just told my brother that kissing me was a mistake."

She let her head rest on the seat back as she stared up at the headliner of the truck, fighting back tears. "It was a mistake for me to go out tonight hoping to reconnect with you. It was a mistake for me not to tell Lance…" She sighed.

He turned toward her. "Not to tell Lance what?"

"Damn this fucking town." She swiped at the tears running down her face. "You really want to know? Fine. I'll tell you. When I came back last summer, I should have told Lance right away that the only reason I came back to town was because I hoped I would see you. All right?"

Tom touched her hand. "Are you serious?"

She covered her face with her hands, embarrassed by the tears streaming from her eyes yet unable to stop them.

Tom leaned across the center console and wrapped an arm around her. "You really are serious?"

She nodded, fighting to breathe evenly, certain he was going to laugh at her. "Just take me home so I can get out of this damn town."

He slipped his hand beneath her hair and caressed the back of her neck. "Come over to my house so we can talk about this."

"I'm not sleeping with you," she muttered, even as her nerves sang beneath his touch.

"Fine. Come over and finish getting drunk. You can pass out on my couch. It'll be fun to have a drinking buddy."

"Doubtful." She folded her hands on her lap and stared out the passenger window. This wasn't what was supposed to happen when she went out with Mira and Keefe. She wasn't supposed to fall all over Tom in the bar or the parking lot where everyone could see her. She'd just wanted to flirt with him a little, maybe catch a ride home with him, and then she would tell him how she felt. Nothing was supposed to happen that would flaunt her feelings in Lance's face.

He reached across the seat and took her hand while continuing to massage her neck.

Kylie tried to remove her hand, but he brought it up to his mouth and blew on it. The hot air warmed more than just her fingers. "Don't," she whispered. Even as she said it, she wondered if sex with Tom would be like it had been when she was fifteen. Or would it be even better?

She couldn't deny her curiosity.

He kissed her knuckle then released her hand and pulled out of the parking lot.

Instead of drawing her hand back, she let it rest on the seat between them. Tom made her feel things she wasn't used to feeling. When she'd been with Lance, it was soothing yet arousing. With Tom, she felt dangerous and needed. It wasn't something she'd felt in years.

"Does that mean you want to come over?" Tom asked as he waited at a stop sign.

Lance clearly wasn't interested in fixing things, and she couldn't remember the last time she'd been falling-down drunk. Tonight was a good night to remedy that. "Sure. Why not?"

They were silent on the way to Tom's house. Kylie kept seeing the pain in Lance's eyes as she stared out the window.

Tom parked the truck in his garage and reached over to squeeze her hand. Kylie pulled away to open her door.

"Come on in." He got out of the truck and opened the door between the garage and house while he waited for her to precede him.

Once inside, she kicked off her boots. "Bring on the booze," she muttered. When she tossed her jacket toward a chair at the kitchen table, she wondered for a moment if she was throwing caution to the wind. It didn't matter. She'd hurt Lance. There was nothing she could do about it tonight. Between the drinking and Tom, at least she wouldn't have to dwell on what a rotten person she was.

"Rum and Coke?" Tom asked as he switched on the lights.

She smoothed her hand over the granite countertop. "You can skip the Coke."

Chapter 18

KYLIE SIPPED A second glass of rum as Tom crouched to light a fire and contemplate the evening. Their kisses had been more than he expected and everything he'd wished for. For a while there, he'd almost hated Lance for interrupting them. But once Kylie had told him the truth in the truck, he'd forgotten everything other than the fact that she'd come back to Chinkapin for him. She had responded to his touch the way she had eleven years ago, but his body's response to touching her was even more potent now. He shifted uncomfortably and turned his attention to the fire. After touching a lit match to a newspaper, he layered kindling over the flame. A few moments later, he added a couple of pieces of firewood.

Satisfied with the fire, he rose, dusted his hands on his jeans, and sat beside her on the sofa. "Need another drink?"

She dropped her head back against the couch. "Doesn't matter."

Tom noted her slurred speech. "Maybe not just yet."

"Yeah, maybe not." She brought her hands up to cover her face and moaned. "I'm pathetic."

"Hardly." He draped his arm around her shoulders and squeezed her. "Why would you even say that?"

She mumbled as she shifted to rest her head on his shoulder. After inhaling the rose and lilac scent of her hair, he sighed. When he was with Kylie, he didn't feel like a man who struggled to walk some days. He didn't feel as though he'd made a lifetime of mistakes, which he could never rectify. Instead, he felt as if he was in high school and had his whole life ahead of him with the girl he loved.

He tipped his head down and brushed his lips over the hair on top of her head. When she didn't move away, he turned and touched her cheek. He guided her face toward his, intent on kissing her.

Noticing her eyes were closed, he froze. "Kylie," he

whispered, shaking her gently.

She didn't respond except to snuggle closer against him.

Realizing she had passed out, he sighed and kissed the top of her head again. No matter how much he wanted to kiss her, he wouldn't while she was passed out. He only wanted her if she chose him as a conscious decision. That didn't mean he was above holding her while she slept, though. He grabbed a blanket from the chest he used as a coffee table and spread it over them.

Kylie sighed and moved her head to his chest. With a groan, Tom shifted backward and to the side, pulling her down next to him. He stroked her hair and imagined what would happen when she woke. He didn't know if she would be happy to be there with him or regret everything, so he focused on the feel of her pressing against him.

His doorbell rang.

"What the…" Sitting up to look over the back of the couch, he saw Eva standing on the porch, holding a small child. He rose, shifting Kylie onto the couch. He pulled the blanket over her, trying to understand why Eva would be on his porch with a kid. She didn't even like kids as far as he knew.

When he opened the door, he didn't mince words. "What are you doing here, Eva?"

"Looking for you, obviously." She smiled, looking up at him through eyelashes that weren't nearly as dark or long as usual. "How are you?"

"I'm fine. Come on in." Tom backed up to let her in as he looked down the driveway, wondering how she got there. There were no extra vehicles parked near the house and no taillights heading down the driveway. Yet, there she was with a kid in her arms and a suitcase at her feet.

Once they were inside, he tried again. "I thought you were skiing with your friends."

"I was, but when I got back to Missoula, you weren't back yet. I figured you were hanging around here, and I missed you, so here I am." She shifted the child enough so Tom could tell it was a girl with curly blond hair, about the age of his nieces. "Can I put her down somewhere? The couch maybe?"

"Not the couch. Come on." He led her to the spare bedroom. Once the kid was tucked in under the designer comforter on the queen-size bed, he turned to Eva. "What's going on?"

"I, uh, got some bad news."

"What's that?" He hoped it was something that would free him from her attentions without him having to hurt her feelings.

"Can we sit down and talk about this?"

He didn't want her in the living room or anywhere that Kylie would notice her if she woke up. That left the bedrooms and bathrooms, which he thought would give Eva the wrong idea. With a sigh, he turned and led her to the kitchen. "I'll make some coffee."

She stood next to him as he started a pot of coffee, but she didn't speak until he was pouring it.

"My ex-husband died."

Tom didn't know she had an ex-husband. "Sorry to hear that."

"My daughter will be living with me."

Tom nearly dropped the cup he held. "That's your daughter?"

Eva took the mug from him and sat at the breakfast bar. "I didn't mention her, did I?"

Tom shook his head. "I didn't even know you had an ex-husband. Why are you telling me now? I told you on the phone that we're done. It was never supposed to be anything serious between us. If I had known you had a kid, I never would have gotten involved with you."

She sighed then turned toward him. "I have a six-year-old daughter, Emily. My ex had custody of her. Now she's moving in with me."

"Wow." He raked a hand through his hair. "I don't know what to say."

Kylie groaned on the sofa.

"What was that?" Eva asked.

"Kylie's passed out on the couch."

"Kylie, your ex? Kylie, your brother's girlfriend?"

"Yes, Kylie, my ex. She and Lance are fighting."

"So she came here?" Her jaw dropped. "Ew."

"Ew?"

"Yeah, that's pretty shitty of her. She hasn't had anything to do with you for years, then she starts dating your brother, and as soon as they have a fight, she runs to you. Probably just to upset Lance."

Tom swallowed. He didn't know how to explain Kylie's presence. He wasn't going to admit that he'd invited her over, hoping to help her forget that Lance had treated her poorly. "Not exactly."

"They're fighting because of you? You're trying to get back with her?"

Tom blew out a deep breath. "Christ, Eva. They were fighting. I ran into Kylie at the bar, and she came over to…"

"To spend the night?"

"I don't know why. Just like I don't really know why you're here with your daughter."

She frowned and narrowed her eyes. "I thought we were pretty serious."

"Really? I didn't think so."

"So I don't mean anything to you?" Her usual tough expression collapsed, turning into that of a pathetic, needy child, which nearly left Tom speechless.

"Of course you mean something to me." He lifted his mug and gestured toward the bottles on the counter. "I've been drinking for a couple hours. Ignore everything I've said. Can we talk about this in the morning when I'm sober?" *After I've had some time to figure out how to let you down more gently?*

He hadn't expected to see her at his house. He definitely had not expected to learn she had a six-year-old kid, but he still wasn't interested in a serious relationship with her. He never had been. Showing up with Emily wasn't going to change his mind.

"Should I leave?"

"Don't be ridiculous. There's plenty of room here." He didn't want to throw her out, even though he didn't really know how the two women would be around each other if Kylie woke up. "How'd you get here, anyway?"

She laughed. "I hitchhiked."

"With a kid?"

"I don't have a car and didn't feel like buying one." She snorted. "And maybe I'm a bit reckless."

"How can you be so reckless with your kid depending on

you?"

"You know what, Tom? If you're going to be a judgmental ass, I can go somewhere else."

"I'm a little stunned. Don't you think that's warranted?"

"Probably."

Tom patted Eva's hand, trying not to be an asshole. "I'm still surprised to see you. I kind of thought when you left Missoula, you were done with me."

"Of course not. I just wanted to go skiing, and I thought you should come home and work on fixing your relationship with your parents."

"Why? What about my parents makes you think they're worth having a relationship with?"

"They're your parents." She sipped from her mug. "You seem different."

"Is that good or bad?" The only difference he felt was that coming back to Chinkapin had given him a chance with Kylie, a chance he didn't want Eva to mess up.

"I'm not sure. Have you seen your family?"

He considered adding a shot of whiskey to his coffee but didn't so he could drive Kylie home later. "It didn't go well."

"How's your search for Erick going?"

"Okay." He couldn't see her expression from the corner of his eye, but she was picking at her cuticles. "Why don't you have custody of your daughter?"

"Didn't. Now I do."

"Did you ever see her?"

"A few times a year."

"And Christmas isn't one of those times?"

She stood. "I'm pretty tired. I think I'll head to bed."

Tom grimaced as he picked up the giant suitcase. It was too much weight for his leg, but he refused to set it back down. "You can sleep in my room if you don't want to share a room with your daughter. I'll crash on the couch."

Her face fell. "Good night."

Thrilled she was letting him postpone any deep conversation, Tom nodded. "Sleep well."

Eva walked through the living room and turned once more to look at him before she disappeared down the hall.

Tom sighed in relief and moved to the couch. A few

minutes later, Kylie groaned and sat up, putting her elbows on her knees and resting her head in her hands.

After crouching in front of her, he reached out to touch her knee, wishing it was bare skin instead of the black stocking things she wore. "You okay?"

She jerked her leg away. "I need to use the bathroom."

Tom rubbed his hands across his face then pointed at the hallway. "Sure. It's the first door on the left." He hoped that Eva was already in one of the bedrooms and that Kylie didn't hear anything from farther down the hall.

Chapter 19

KYLIE PUSHED OPEN the bathroom door and froze. On the edge of the bathtub, Eva sat weeping quietly. "Oh. Sorry. I didn't realize anyone was in here." She backed up and began pulling the door closed but froze. "Are you okay?"

Eva waved her hand dismissively. "I'll be fine. Not that anyone around here cares."

Kylie stepped forward. "What's going on? Does Tom know you're here?"

"Yeah, he knows. He just doesn't care." Eva took a swig from the bottle next to her. "Want a drink?"

Kylie shook her head. "No, I've had enough for tonight. Maybe even too much."

"Tom said you're fighting with Lance."

Unsure of where Tom and Eva's relationship stood, Kylie nodded. "Yeah. Lance is having a hard time accepting that Tom and I have a past to deal with."

Eva swiped at her nose with a tissue. "You mean Erick?"

"Yeah." Kylie leaned against the doorframe. "When I told my mom I was pregnant, they hustled me off to a school for pregnant teens. A few days after Erick was born, the nurses told me he had died of pneumonia. Last summer when I came back here, I found out—with Lance's help—that Erick hadn't died and someone adopted him. Tom probably told you all of that already, though."

"Wait. Lance helped you?"

"Yeah, he went to Middleton with me and tried to help me find records. We didn't find anything definitive, but we found enough to figure out that they'd lied about Erick dying."

Eva wrinkled her nose. "So he helped you learn Erick was alive and now doesn't want you to find him and have a relationship?"

"I don't know what he thinks about me having a relationship with Erick. He just doesn't seem to understand that Tom and I have a past and we're trying to find Erick. We're always going to have a past, even if Lance doesn't like it."

Eva took another drink. "I know how Lance feels."

"How so?"

"Tom's obsessed with you, Kylie. He's still in love with you."

Kylie rubbed her face. A few hours ago, she would have been thrilled to hear that Tom still loved her. Now, she didn't know how to process the information. "I doubt that. I think he just wants me to help him find Erick."

Eva pressed her lips together in a humorless grin. "I know how you feel. I hope you'll understand how I feel."

"About what?" Kylie crossed her arms.

"I'm pregnant, Kylie. With Tom's baby. You can't keep him from me."

Kylie looked over her shoulder to see if Tom had come to look for her. "You're what?"

"Pregnant, and I don't have anyone to help me." She offered Kylie the bottle, and this time, Kylie took it.

She took three deep swallows before she handed it back with a grimace. "Should you be drinking if you're pregnant?"

Eva shrugged. "I got pregnant right before Tom left Montana to come see you. He told me it was to work things out with his parents, but I know it was just to see you. He doesn't care enough about his parents to fix their relationship."

Kylie shook her head. "I don't have anything to do with this, Eva. I didn't ask him to come back here. I didn't even want to come back myself. I only did it for Lance."

"I want this baby. Tom's baby. I made lots of mistakes with my first baby, but I'm not going to with this one."

"You have another child?"

Eva nodded and gestured toward the hallway. "Yeah, she's sleeping over there. She's six. When my parents found out I was pregnant, they told me that I was too selfish to be a mother and too busy having a good time. They refused to help me, and since I was technically an adult, I told them off and married Emily's father."

Kylie could barely speak, but she managed to choke out, "What happened?"

"Emily had colic for six months straight. My husband was working two jobs to support us, and I thought I was losing my mind. So I left. I left my husband and Emily so I could go out and party. I've spent the past six years partying."

"You didn't have your daughter, though."

"Nope. Not until I got a call a week ago from my mom saying that Emily's dad died and I had to come get her."

Kylie turned away. "I have to go." She couldn't listen to any more of Eva's story, but it was clear that she couldn't act on her attraction to Tom. She'd thrown away her relationship with Lance for a few kisses with a man who was about to have a baby with another woman.

Chapter 20

As Tom started the truck, Kylie stared out the window. "Are you and Eva still dating?"

Tom slowed at the end of his driveway then pulled onto the road. "She went to Colorado, and I came home. I thought it was over."

"Well, she must not think it's over. She showed up on your doorstep with her kid."

"Yeah. I guess." Eva showing up didn't make any sense to Tom. They weren't together, but he didn't want to disrespect Eva by telling Kylie that she just couldn't accept they were through.

They were both silent for a minute or two until Kylie finally spoke. "Just take me back to the bar. I'll get my truck and drive myself home."

"You've been drinking."

"I can catch a ride with someone."

"You're not driving. I said I'd drive you home. I will."

Kylie pulled her jacket closer and crossed her arms.

Tom glanced at her as he slowed to turn onto the road by her house. "You know, nothing happened."

"We kissed."

"I meant nothing happened at my house. You fell asleep."

After a couple of minutes of silence, Tom cleared his throat. "So, I guess I fucked up any chance of you and I being friends."

She rubbed her temples. "I don't know."

"I'm sorry. I'll clear things up with Eva when I get back."

"What does 'clear things up with Eva' mean?"

"I'll make it clear that we're through, that I'm only letting her stay because we're friends. I mean, she took care of me in Montana when I could barely stand up. I owe her."

"You do. You owe her the truth and loyalty. I never would have kissed you tonight if I'd known you were still with her."

"I'm not 'with her.' She showed up, needing a place to stay."

Kylie sighed. She couldn't fault him for letting Eva and her daughter stay at his house. Kylie had no claim on him. She just felt awful for kissing another woman's man. Even if Tom wasn't dating Eva, Eva loved him, and she was pregnant with Tom's baby. "You need to straighten things out with Eva."

"I will, but she's probably asleep by now. Are we still friends?"

"Who? Me and you?" Kylie smiled. "Don't be ridiculous. Of course we're still friends."

When Tom pulled up to Kylie's house, he turned toward her. He wanted to walk her to the door and kiss her until she invited him in. He had no issues with kissing his brother's ex. She'd been his ex first.

Clearly, Lance didn't love Kylie if he had let her go so easily. He couldn't expect to have a future with her if he couldn't accept her past was with Tom. It had nearly killed Tom when he found out Lance was dating Kylie. When he had heard about Lance and Kylie, he had gone out to the river where he and Kylie had first met. After drinking way too much, he'd slipped as he was walking along the river. He'd barely been able to limp back to his truck, where he'd slept that night.

Since Kylie had returned to Chinkapin last spring, Tom's tolerance for alcohol had tripled, at least—maybe even more than that. Regardless of his drinking problem, he hoped they would be able to move on. Maybe he would be able to quit drinking and get on with his life.

"You know how you said you think Mira and Keefe were meant to be together?" he asked, unwilling to end his time with Kylie. Even if he couldn't kiss her, he still loved spending time with her.

"Yeah."

"What about you and Lance?"

"What about us?"

"Are you guys meant to be together?"

She looked out the window. "I should let you get back to Eva."

"It can wait." He wasn't looking forward to talking to Eva. Being blunt with Eva was the most honorable thing to do, and now that he'd made that decision, he wanted to put it off a bit longer. "What are you up to?"

"Probably sitting around sketching."

He was surprised that she didn't plan on just going to bed. "What are you working on?"

"It's stupid," she muttered.

"I doubt that."

"I was drawing Erick." She bit her fingernail. "It's what I do every year. I draw a picture of him like I see him in my head. Opening Christmas presents or sitting under the tree."

Tom watched her wipe her fingers under her eyes, and he wanted to erase all of her sadness. He knew that wouldn't be welcomed. Maybe it would have been earlier before Lance had spotted them kissing, but it was clear now that she wasn't interested in him. "You miss him."

"Of course I miss him."

"And you love him."

"Was there ever any doubt about that?"

"No." He touched her hand. "I wish things were different."

After a moment of silence, Kylie turned her hand over to twine her fingers with his. "I do too, but there's nothing we can do about the past."

"There's always the future."

"Back to the future, huh?"

Maybe she wasn't so against them being together. Maybe she realized that Lance wasn't as wonderful as she'd thought. Maybe he'd misread the situation. "Can I see your drawings?"

After studying him for a few seconds, she nodded.

By the time he rounded the front of the truck, Kylie was halfway up the porch steps. After she unlocked the door and pushed it open, she gestured for him to go inside.

Tom stepped into the dark house. When she reached behind him to switch on the light, she brushed against him. He didn't know if it was on purpose or accident, but he turned away, removing his jacket and hanging it on the coat tree.

Kylie left her boots on the boot tray then walked away, switching on lights as she made her way to the kitchen. Tom quickly removed his boots and followed her. When he stepped into the brightly lit kitchen, she was peering into the fridge. She reached for something then straightened and closed the fridge, empty-handed. "Want some coffee?"

"Is that what you want?"

She shook her head. "I was going to have a beer, but…"

"But didn't think you should encourage my drinking?"

"More like I've probably had enough to drink today." She smiled. "And I don't want to encourage your drinking."

"Why?"

"Because I'm worried about you."

He stepped forward and lowered his voice, surprised that she'd nearly admitted she still cared about him. "You care about me?"

"Of course I care about you, Tom. Don't be silly." She started a pot of coffee.

He moved closer while her back was turned. "Just like you care about any random stranger?"

She glanced over her shoulder and rolled her eyes. When she turned around, she leaned back, hands resting on the counter at her sides. "You drink a lot." Her fingers tapped silently on the countertop.

"Why does everyone keep saying that?"

"Because we all care about you? Or maybe because your brother is constantly driving you home because you're drunk?"

"Constantly? He's only had to drive me home when I visited my parents. They bring out the best in me."

"What's with you guys?"

"What do you mean?"

Kylie filled two stoneware cups and handed one to Tom. "I don't know. I'm just trying to work my nerve up to show you the drawings."

"Why? What's so hard about showing me?"

She sighed and met his gaze. "I thought you knew how I feel about my drawing."

He smiled, proud of himself for knowing. "Is it still like baring your soul?"

She nodded. "And when the subject is Erick, it's even more…"

"Scary? Nerve-wracking? Heart-breaking?"

"Yeah. That about covers it." She walked over to the kitchen table and pulled out a chair, but instead of sitting down, she pushed it back in. "Come on," she said over her shoulder before walking down the hall.

Tom followed her, gaze fixed on her legs as they climbed up to the attic and she switched on the light. He looked around the nearly empty room. Next to the window was a big armchair and a side table. On the table were a cup of pencils and a couple of sketchbooks. She wasn't the only one nervous about the drawings. Tom had only seen one picture of Erick as a newborn. He'd imagined many times what his son might look like and was curious how his imagination matched up to Kylie's.

After padding over to the table and picking up one of the books, she flipped pages before handing it to him and moving away to stand in front of the window. She folded her arms around her waist and watched him.

On the page in the opened sketchbook was an intricate sketch of the fifteen-year-old Kylie he remembered. She was standing in front of a Christmas tree, holding a baby. She gazed down at the baby in her arms, love apparent on her face. Next to her, stood…

He drew his gaze away from the picture and met her eyes. "Me?"

Tears ran down her face, but she didn't try to hide them or wipe them away as she nodded.

"Why?"

"Why do you think? I was in love with you. I wanted our family. You, me, and Erick." She pushed her hair back behind her ear. "It was my Christmas wish for quite a while."

His heart seemed to stop. He'd wished for the same thing until the rumor that she'd had an abortion got back to him, and then she hadn't come back to Chinkapin for her sophomore year of high school. "And now?"

"Now, I just wish for him to be happy." She turned away to stare at the black window, and he wondered if she could see anything outside or just his reflection as he looked at the drawing.

"Is this the one you were working on this year?"

"No. That was the first one. I thought you'd want to see all of them."

"What if it just makes me miserable?"

"There's that possibility. So don't look."

"But I want to see him."

"I don't know what he looks like, Tom. I know what he looked like when he was born. I know what he looked like when he was three days old." She turned sideways, enough that he could see her brow wrinkle and the corners of her mouth turn down. "I don't know what he looks like now."

"Do you want to know what he looks like? I want to meet him."

"Yeah, I told you I wanted to find him. I just don't want to mess up his life."

"What if his life already is messed up, and he wants to know us?"

"Then he needs to initiate that search. I'm not willing to chance messing up his life."

"What if he's abused? What if he doesn't know he's adopted? What if he hates the people who adopted him and has no way to find us?"

Her gaze darted around the room, and she twisted her hands together. "Why do you have to look for the worst in everything? I've had eleven years to think about this. He has to be in a good home. I couldn't live with myself if he wasn't."

Unwilling to push her when she looked so helpless, he set his stoneware mug on the side table and held up the sketchbook in question. "May I look at the others?"

She nodded. "Sure."

He flipped through the next nine sketches, noting that he quit appearing in them at the fifth one. Kylie quit appearing in them in year eight.

"So you gave up on your fantasy of our complete family when he was five?"

"I came to terms with it the fifth Christmas after he was born."

He turned to the picture she was working on, which showed her and a boy sitting in front of a Christmas tree. Behind them, with a hand on each of their shoulders, was him. He smiled in happiness. She'd been thinking of him, and clearly, she'd been thinking of him and Erick with her. "And how do you explain this?"

She sighed. "It's a fantasy. Not reality. Besides, it's possible that we could all be part of each other's lives without tearing him from the family he knows."

"And you're willing to do that?"

She grabbed a sweatshirt and pulled it on. "That would be the closest I'd want to be involved in his life."

Somehow, Kylie could pull off the look of an oversized sweatshirt with ratty cuffs over a slim-fitting dress. Tom tried not to focus on her beauty. "Don't you want to be his mother?"

"I don't want to be anyone's mother, especially Erick's."

"Why don't you want to be anyone's mother?" She was so caring and clearly loved the boy.

"Why do you want to talk about this?"

"Why don't you want to talk about this?"

"It's over and done with, Tom. Why keep discussing the same thing? Just let it go."

Unable to look at the drawing any longer, he closed the sketchbook and set it on the table beside his mug. "I can't. I never got to meet him. I deserve at least that."

"Really? How are you going to prove that you deserve it? Are you going to have a judge order every ten-year-old boy who was adopted to have DNA testing done to compare to yours?"

"I don't think that'll be necessary. I have an investigator looking for him, but if I have to beg a judge for multiple DNA tests, I will. I want to find my son."

Her eyes dropped to the floor. "That's ridiculous," she whispered. "You're being ridiculous."

"I want to find my son," he repeated as he clenched and unclenched his fists. Then he shook his hands, hoping the tension would leave his body.

Kylie shook her head. "This was a mistake. I shouldn't have invited you in. I never should have thought we'd agree on this."

Tom glanced at the sketch again. It resembled the picture he'd imagined too. He didn't know how to explain it to her, but he sure as hell was going to give it a shot. He gripped her shoulders and gazed into her eyes. "I hated being a Mallock. My entire life, people have treated me a certain way because of my last name. They don't bother getting to know me for me."

"That's not true. I got to know you. I never expected to come upon a Mallock fishing in the river, though. I'm not sure I would have gotten to know you if I'd known. I'd heard too many stories from my parents about how awful your family is."

"See? Right there. You're confirming what I just said."

She tried to shrug from beneath his hands.

"Kylie, you are the only person who loved me for being me. I miss that. I want that back."

"I'm not the only person who could love you, Tom. What about Eva? She seemed pretty sincere."

He waved his hand in dismissal and turned away, running a hand through his hair. "She just wanted to have a good time. We both just wanted to have a good time when we started seeing each other. She's not someone I could spend my life with."

"Really? You know that? How?"

"Because. She wanted me to come home for Christmas, even knowing how pissed I was at my family."

The color from Kylie's face drained. "What's wrong with wanting you to patch things up with your parents? Or at least start to?"

"She didn't give a shit about why I came home; she just didn't want me to sit in Missoula all alone. She wanted to go skiing with friends and felt guilty leaving me by myself."

"Maybe because she cares about you."

"Maybe. Or maybe she realized that I loved someone else. You."

Kylie backed away, shaking her head, her green eyes wide. "You don't love me, Tom. You can't love me. You don't even know me anymore."

Tom stepped forward. "What about that kiss? That was more than just a casual kiss. You have to admit that."

There wasn't anywhere for Kylie to back up. "I don't have to admit anything."

He lowered his face toward her, inhaling her scent of roses and lilacs, and wrapped a lock of her hair around his finger. "Did you kiss Lance like that?"

Kylie blinked and shook her head angrily. "I'm not answering that. You need to leave."

"Why?"

"Because I don't want to have this conversation with you."

"Do you want to kiss me instead?"

She swallowed, touched her tongue to her lower lip, then

shoved past him to head down the attic stairs. "No," she said over her shoulder.

Tom followed, cursing himself. He shouldn't have pushed her.

When they got to the front door, Kylie crossed her arms, refusing to meet his gaze.

After he put his boots on, Tom touched her shoulder. "I'm sorry."

She jerked away as if his hand was a hot coal. "Just go," she whispered.

"Please, don't do this."

"Don't do what? Throw you out? Tell you to leave me the hell alone? Insist you leave Erick alone?" She tossed her hair back. "What exactly is it that you don't want me to do?"

"Don't be pissed at me. Don't let my mistake ruin this."

"Which mistake, Tom? Spell it out for me. I want to know exactly what it is you want me to forget happened."

"You don't have to forget anything. I just want you to forgive me for pressing the issue. Or is it bringing Lance up that I should apologize for?"

Kylie pulled the door open and handed Tom his jacket. "Both."

"Then I'm sorry for both of those."

Kylie's green eyes met his. After a moment, she nodded. "Forgiven."

"Thank you." Tom stepped out of the house, and she shut the door behind him. When he got to his truck, he looked back. All the lights were off in the house, even the attic light.

"I guess I fucked that up," he muttered as he started the truck and left. He considered going back to the bar and picking a fight with Scott, just because he was in a horrid mood, but instead he went home. Kylie was right about one thing—he owed Eva an honest discussion about why they were through.

* * *

When Tom walked into his house, he was surprised to see Eva sitting at the kitchen table. "What's up? I thought you were tired and going to bed."

"We need to talk."

"I had to drive Kylie home. I thought we decided to wait

until tomorrow to talk."

She raised an eyebrow. "You're not drunk, Tom. We can talk now."

"It's late, though."

"Nice try." She pointed at the chair across the table.

Tom swallowed and nodded, hoping that she would tell him they weren't going to be dating anymore. "Okay, what's up?"

She met his gaze evenly. "I'm pregnant."

Tom blinked, wiggled a finger in his ear, and mumbled, "Huh?"

"You heard me."

"But…" They'd only had sex the one time since his accident. "I thought you were on something. How can you be pregnant?"

"Apparently, we're part of the one percent failure rate of IUDs."

"Are you sure?"

"Yes. I saw a doctor a couple of days ago. It's still early, but I'm pregnant."

He dropped his head to his hands. "How the hell can this be happening?" he muttered.

"Look, I'm not happy about it, either. Especially when I found out you were trying to get back with Kylie."

"I'm not trying to get back with Kylie. I'm trying to be friends with her because I hope she'll help me find Erick." It wasn't completely a lie, but he admitted to himself that it wasn't completely true, either.

"Well, you have another kid besides Erick to think about now." Her grin made him wonder if she'd done this on purpose, hoping it would make him more interested in her.

As the news sank in, Tom's stomach twisted.

"Are you mad?"

Tom considered it for a moment before he answered. "Why would I be mad? You know how much I want Erick."

She nodded cautiously. "I guess I just wasn't sure whether you wanted Erick or his mother."

"I want Erick, and I want this baby."

Eva yawned before laughing. "I was so scared to tell you. I was afraid you'd be angry at me. Like I'd done it on purpose."

Tom leaned back and crossed his arms. "Did you?"

She shook her head. "You really think I'd do that?"

When she yawned again, Tom gestured toward the bedroom. "You should get some sleep. We'll talk more in the morning."

"Are you coming to bed with me to celebrate?"

Tom sank onto the couch. "Not right now." There was no way he could sleep, and he wasn't interested in having sex with her. Last time he'd given in, he had apparently impregnated her, and now he would be connected to her for the rest of his life. Just when he thought things were going his way with Kylie, Eva had to show up. He'd even been convinced that once he made it clear he and Eva were through, Kylie would be interested in him again.

But now, things were just fucked up. He picked up the rum he'd brought into the living room a few hours ago and uncapped it to gulp from the bottle.

Chapter 21

KYLIE WOKE UP on New Year's Day with a sour stomach and a dry mouth. Even though she'd drunk too much the previous night, her uneasy feeling was more mental than physical.

When she heard a knock at the door, she grimaced. "God, I hope that's not Tom."

She pulled open the door, relieved to see Lance leaning against the porch railing, looking perfectly calm and relaxed.

"Hey, come on in. I'll make some coffee."

He nodded and followed her in, but as she started to make the coffee, he stopped her. "I didn't come over here for coffee."

"Oh. What did you come over for?"

He took a single key from his pocket and laid it on the counter. "I don't need this anymore."

"Can we still be friends?"

"I don't think so."

Kylie picked up the key and dropped it in the silverware drawer. "I don't want you to be mad at me."

"I have a right to be mad at you. You were making out with my brother."

"You and I weren't together."

He glared at her. "Only because you told me to leave."

"And you left. You didn't argue with me about that at all." If he was going to be so upset that she'd kissed someone else, why hadn't he tried to change her mind about kicking him out?

"You knew what you wanted. I gave it to you."

"I wanted you to trust me, dammit. What's so hard to understand about that?"

"I don't want to be your second choice," he said.

"You're not." She wiped at the tear that snuck out of her eye. "He was my second choice. You're my first choice."

"He was your first. He'll always be your first."

Frustrated that it kept returning to the distant past, Kylie wanted to punch something. "That's the whole problem, isn't it? You don't care at all how many people I've had sex with; the only one that matters is Tom. Right?"

"No, I don't care at all anymore. You can sleep with whoever you want." He opened the door, and she followed him onto the porch. "We're not together. Remember?"

Pressing her lips together, she watched as his Jeep drove away from her for the second time in less than twelve hours. This time, she wasn't going to ask for forgiveness. Clearly, they weren't meant to be together, and whether he admitted it or not, he just didn't care about her enough to understand Tom would always be a part of her past.

* * *

Forty-five minutes later, Kylie got out of Keefe's truck at the bar. "Thanks for the ride."

After he nodded and left the parking lot, she stepped inside the entrance and paused to let her eyes adjust to the dim light. As she approached the bar, she questioned the intelligence of this. "As if it could make things any worse," she muttered under her breath. Once she could see, she was surprised by how empty the bar was. She'd expected a bigger lunch crowd, but nobody was in the stale-beer-scented room.

After settling on a bar stool, she waited.

"What can I get…" Her brother's voice faded away along with his customary smile when he spotted her.

"Can we talk?" she asked.

"I don't know what we have to talk about." He glanced at his watch then tugged at his beard. "I'm waiting on a delivery. Maybe another day."

Kylie took a deep breath and clenched her fists together on her lap beneath the bar. "This will just take a minute."

"Suit yourself." Scott wiped down the bar top with a rag as Kylie waited for him to meet her gaze. When he didn't even bother moving to the end of the bar where she sat, she realized she probably couldn't change his mind about her. All talking to her younger brother would accomplish was making her feel better because she would know she had tried. After her conversation with Lance, she wasn't sure anything could make her feel better.

"I'm sorry if you feel like I forgot you when I went to Middleton. I didn't leave by choice, and I certainly didn't know Kristy had died."

He shrugged. "It doesn't matter."

"Then what is it? Why do you hate me? Why won't you even talk to me?" She wanted to reach out and pull him into a hug the way she had every time he'd been angry with her before she'd left, before he hated her.

He curled his lip into a sneer. "You're clearly better than me. No sense wasting your time talking to me."

"That's ridiculous, Scott. I loved you. I still love you. You're my brother. I was devastated to be sent away when I told Mom I was pregnant, but at least I thought I'd still have you and Kristy when I came back. Except Kristy was gone, and you've barely talked to me since. I was in here less than a week ago, trying to talk to you, and you didn't have time. Yet last night, you had time to badmouth me to Tom Mallock."

"I'm not ten anymore, Kylie. You have your own life. Just leave me alone." A bell rang behind the bar, and he jerked his head toward the back door. "I have to go."

Kylie nodded as he walked away without a glance in her direction. Sighing, she buttoned her coat and went out to start her truck.

She didn't know which hurt worse, being rejected by Lance or being rejected by her own brother. She turned the key, and the truck roared to life. Feeling sorry for herself, she let the engine warm up for a couple of minutes then turned toward home. Now, she had no one. She couldn't—wouldn't—pursue a relationship with Tom, knowing that Eva was pregnant. Lance wouldn't be her friend because she'd had sex with Tom twelve years ago. Her younger brother wouldn't even talk to her because she hadn't known Kristy died while she was in Middleton.

Chapter 22

THREE DAYS LATER, Tom woke in the morning to find Emily standing next to the couch. "Where's my mom?"

"In bed."

"No. She's not here. Where is she?"

"I don't know, kiddo. I just woke up." Tom rubbed his head. The night before, he'd drunk more bourbon than he should have. He had thought it would help him sleep, but it hadn't. His dreams had been riddled with images of Kylie and Erick next to a Christmas tree. After every dream, he would jerk awake, eager to hurt his parents for stealing Erick.

When he'd gone back to sleep, he'd dreamt it again and again.

"She left me here with you. Where did she go?"

"Maybe she had to run to the store."

"With her suitcase?"

Tom peered at the girl with dark-blond curls. "What are you talking about?"

"She slept in that bedroom." Emily pointed at Tom's room. "But she's not there, and her suitcase is gone too."

No way. She wouldn't just leave her kid with me without asking. Would she? Tom sat up, drawing the quilt around his waist. "How about you go into the kitchen and see what you want for breakfast? I'll get dressed and look for your mom while you eat. Okay?"

Emily walked slowly into the kitchen, watching Tom over her shoulder as he stood. He kept the blanket wrapped around his waist, trying to remember why he thought it was a good idea to sleep on the couch in the nude when there were other people in his house—people who apparently thought it was just fine to disappear and leave their child alone with him.

After dressing in his bedroom, he walked into the kitchen.

Emily held a piece of paper out to him. "Here."

Tom took it, glanced at it, frowned, and leaned against the

counter to read it.

Tom, I have to take care of some stuff. Please keep Emily safe. I'll be back as soon as possible. ~Eva

"What the hell?" he muttered.

"You can't say that."

"Can't say what?"

She stood in front of him, arms crossed, tapping her stockinged foot. "Swears."

Tom thought for a second, trying to figure out what he'd said. "Hell? That's a swear?"

Emily nodded.

"Sorry. I'll try to remember not to say it."

She pointed at the paper he held. "Is that from my mom?"

"Yeah."

"What's it say?"

"That she had to go take care of some stuff, and she'll be back as soon as possible."

"What stuff?"

"I don't know." He really wished he had an answer for the girl with curly blond hair. Hell, he wished he had an answer for himself. Right now, he wished he'd never opened the door for Eva the other night, but where would Emily be now if he hadn't? It was clear Eva wasn't fit to be a mother.

"What else did she say?"

"That's it."

Her lower lip quivered as she hugged herself. "Did she say anything to me?"

He crumpled the paper and stuffed it in his pocket as he crouched down. "She said to tell you she loves you to pieces, and I'm supposed to give you a big hug from her."

"Really?"

Tom nodded and wrapped the girl in his arms. He didn't want the tears in her eyes to fall, so he rose and spun in a circle until she laughed. "Now, what do you want for breakfast?"

"Toast and dippy eggs."

"What are dippy eggs?"

"Eggs that you can dip your toast in."

"Dippy eggs it is. Can you get the eggs out of the fridge?" He grimaced and rubbed at his leg. Crouching and spinning hadn't helped anything other than Emily's mood, but her laughter was worth the pain.

After breakfast, Tom and Emily were just finishing an episode of Bugs Bunny when he noticed the tears pooled in her eyes. "It'll be okay. Your mom will be back as soon as she can be."

Emily's lip trembled, and she buried her face in her hands. "I miss my daddy. I want him."

Tom moved to hug her. "I know. I'm sure he misses you too." He was surprised that she didn't cry for her mother, but it made sense. It sounded as though she barely knew her mother.

He racked his brain trying to find something to distract her from her misery. He didn't know much about dolls or kids' toys, so he was stumped until he remembered the box of toys his sisters' kids played with at his parents' house. "Do you like dogs?"

"Yeah. I want one, but Daddy said we couldn't have one in our apartment."

"Oh? Should we go visit some dogs?" If it would make Emily happy, he would visit his parents.

"Yeah!" Her smile was the deal breaker.

The scar on Tom's leg twitched as he drove to his parents' house with Emily beside him. He probably should have called first, but he didn't want to argue. Right now, he didn't even want to punish them. He just wanted to entertain Emily for a while.

He pulled into the driveway and parked in front of the two-story log home. "Here we are. Let's go see if we can find some dogs." He took a deep breath and opened his door. His parents' two golden retrievers were by his side before he rounded the truck to help Emily out.

"You're good at finding dogs." She reached for the closest one. "What's her name?"

"Ishy, and that one is Yucky. My nephews named them."

"Hi, there," she said and hugged the dog who sat down and looked at Tom with his tongue lolling out.

Hazel spoke from the porch with a smile. "Hello, Tom. I certainly didn't expect to see you when the dogs started barking."

Tom nodded. "Understandable. I just brought Emily over because she likes dogs. I didn't think you'd mind."

Hazel raised an eyebrow but shook her head. "Of course not. Come on inside." When Emily and the dogs stepped on the porch, Hazel greeted her warmly. "Hi there, dear. I'm Tom's mom. You can call me Hazel."

"Hello." Emily reached for Tom's hand, and he felt his heart melt.

"Emily is Eva's daughter. She's staying with me for a few days while Eva is busy."

"I see. Shall we go in the kitchen and have some hot cocoa?"

Emily nodded but stayed next to Tom until they were inside. Once in the kitchen with Hazel focused on making hot cocoa, Emily crouched down by the dogs' beds and petted the spoiled retrievers. Tom could see her lips moving as she talked to the dogs, but he couldn't hear what she said.

Hazel glanced over her shoulder at Tom as he settled into a chair at the table. "How long is Emily staying with you?"

"Until Eva comes back."

"And that will be?"

Tom shrugged. "A few days." He hoped it wasn't going to be more than a few days. Even though he liked kids and wanted custody of Erick, he didn't have any experience taking care of kids. He was the uncle who liked playing with his nieces and nephews while they were happy. As soon as they were anything other than happy, he left the room.

Hazel pressed her lips together, and Tom knew she was biting her tongue for Emily's sake. After smiling in gratitude at her discretion, he cleared his throat. "I was actually wondering if Ishy and Yucky would like to have a sleepover at my house."

Hazel nodded. "Sure. I bet they'd love it."

"Who would love what?" Lance asked, rubbing his face as he entered the kitchen.

Tom blinked in surprise. It was clear from Lance's sleepy expression that he'd moved back into his old bedroom when Kylie threw him out, and he obviously hadn't slept much last night. "The dogs are going to stay with Emily and I for a bit."

"Already done kissing Kylie and moving on to someone named Emily?" Lance grumbled.

"Lance!" Hazel gestured at the girl in the corner.

Tom clenched his fists and glared at Lance. "Emily is

staying with me for a bit while her mom is out of town."

"Oh." Lance's face turned red, and he smiled at the girl watching him from the blue plaid dog bed. "Hi. I'm Tom's brother, Lance."

"Hello," she whispered before focusing her attention back on the dogs, who watched her raptly.

Lance poured a cup of coffee and sat across from Tom. "Who's her mom?" he asked in a low voice.

"Eva."

"Yours?"

Tom shook his head, astounded Lance would even ask that. Did Lance somehow know that Eva was pregnant with his baby? "Can you stop over later today? I want to talk to you about something." He'd hoped Lance would help him figure out how to find Eva, but obviously he was still pissed about catching Tom and Kylie kissing on New Year's Eve.

Lance shifted his gaze away. "I don't think so."

"Look, it was a mistake, but it was all me. Don't blame Kylie."

Apparently unwilling to spend more than a few seconds in Tom's presence, Lance stood. "Thanks for the coffee, Mom. I'll see you after work."

After Lance left the room, Tom turned to Hazel. "He's staying here?"

"Yes, it's nice having him home. He's looking for an apartment but hasn't told me what happened with Kylie."

"Does it matter? Aren't you just happy he's not with her anymore?"

Hazel poured three cups of cocoa and set them on the table. "No. Believe it or not, I actually prefer for my children to be happy. He was happy with Kylie."

Tom bit back his response. He wasn't ready to forgive Hazel yet. "Come on over and drink your cocoa, Emily."

Once the little girl settled next to Tom, Hazel carried the conversation with her. Tom just sat there, wondering where the hell Eva had gone and what the hell he was going to do about it.

* * *

Just as Tom and Emily were putting their shoes on to leave

his parents' house, his phone rang.

"Hello," he answered while watching Emily and the dogs. All three stared at him. He suspected Emily was hoping her mom was calling. He wasn't sure what the dogs expected from a phone call—maybe that the pizza place on the south end of town had made too many pizzas and wanted to deliver them to him. He hoped like hell it was Eva and that she was at his house, wondering where he and Emily were.

"Hi, Tom. This is Dick Sorenson, the investigator you hired. I've made some progress on your case."

"Great. What kind of progress?" Tom hoped the investigator had narrowed it down to a couple of different leads in trying to locate Erick's adoptive parents.

"I'm ninety percent convinced I've found him. He was adopted at the right time from Middleton, he has reddish brown hair and green eyes, and his name is Erick."

Tom's heart skipped, but he forced himself to remain calm. "That doesn't really mean anything. Lots of people have the name Erick."

"True enough. I have a feeling, though."

"That's great." Tom leaned forward in the chair then stood. After covering the phone with his hand, he spoke to Emily. "I'll be right back. If you need anything, I'll be in the other room, okay?"

After Emily nodded, Tom rushed from the room. "Where is he? When will you know if it's him?"

"He's actually in a foster home right now."

"What? That can't be him. Someone adopted my son. Why would my son be in a foster home?"

"It appears that this child's parents died recently in a car accident."

Tom pinched the bridge of his nose. "When did his parents die? What about his relatives?"

"A year ago. I'm not sure yet why he's not with relatives. I've been in contact with the child's social worker. She agreed right away to submit DNA to find out if he's your son."

"When will we know?"

"That's why I'm calling. I have the results and would like to meet with you and Miss Killian tomorrow to discuss them."

Tom nodded. "And if it is him? Then what?"

"Then we file for custody." They were both silent for a few seconds before the investigator spoke. "That is what you want, right?"

Tom nodded. He wanted custody but didn't know how Eva was going to play into it. If she didn't come back, would he be able to gain custody of Erick with an abandoned child living in his house? "Of course. I just… I can't believe that my son might be coming home to me soon. It seems way too easy."

"I told you that I always find my subject, didn't I?"

"Of course. I just thought that was propaganda BS. I didn't know you actually meant it."

"Sure, I meant it, and you know that because you checked me out pretty thoroughly before hiring me. We both know you'd never settle for second best."

"Right." Tom's mind was on how Kylie would react to the news. He hoped she would be as excited as he was.

"Look, I appreciate all your work on this, and I have another project for you."

"What kind of project?"

"A woman I dated a while back showed up here the other night with her six-year-old daughter. This morning, she disappeared, leaving her daughter here. I need to find her. Can you find her?"

"I can try. Email me everything you know about her, and I'll get started right away."

"Great. Thanks." They made plans to meet before Tom ended the call and returned to the living room, where Emily was playing with the dogs again. "Everything okay?"

She smiled at him with obvious relief on her face. "Fine."

With a deep sigh, he gestured for his mother to come over. "Mom, I need some help. I need someone to watch Emily for a little while so I can go talk to Kylie."

"Is everything okay?"

"Yeah. I just need to talk to her." He was willing to ask his mother for help even though they'd never had the conversation they'd discussed on Christmas Eve, but he wasn't willing to confide in her yet. Once he knew for sure that he'd found his son, he would tell his parents.

"What's going on, Thomas? Why is that little girl staying with you?"

"Eva's ex-husband died, and Emily will be living with Eva."

"Then where is Eva?"

Tom lowered his voice. "I don't know." He told her about the note.

Hazel pressed her lips together and frowned. "How could a mother just leave her child?"

He didn't want to agree with her. He didn't want to tell her he'd asked the same question a thousand times since waking up that morning. "She left her phone on the nightstand in the bedroom. I called everyone that I know of who she considers a friend. I even tried to find her parents, but Emily doesn't know much about them to help me find them. We don't know what's going on, Mom. We shouldn't judge Eva until we know why she left or where she went."

"Did you get any advice from Lance?"

"You saw him. He won't talk to me."

"Why? What did you do?"

"Come on, Mom. Why do you always assume I did something? Even when we were kids, you always took Lance's side. You never believed me that Lance was the one who started that fire in the backyard."

"He was four."

"A four-year-old firebug with a magnifying glass." He took a deep breath and let it out. "Lance is upset about the time Kylie's been spending with me." Telling her that much was easier than denying he'd had anything to do with Lance moving back in with his parents. "We're trying to find Erick."

"Well, there's nothing wrong with that."

Tom narrowed his eyes, wondering if he'd heard correctly. "You think we should find Erick?"

"I think it's normal and natural. We shouldn't have done what we did, Tom. We realize that now, but you have to realize that as parents, all we wanted to do was protect you guys."

"From what, Mom? My responsibilities? My son?" He met Hazel's gaze and held it, until she looked down at her hands twisting together. "I loved Kylie. I would have married her and taken care of Erick."

"Your life would have been different. It wouldn't have been easy, honey."

"It doesn't matter. Erick was mine. Kylie was mine. It was

our life to live, easy or not. Our decision to make, not yours and not her parents'."

Hazel patted his hand. "I know, and I understand that you're still upset. I'd really like it if you could at least let your father and me still be part of your life. Not just when you need something from us, but just because we do love you."

Tom gave a curt nod. "I'll try harder to forgive you, but I can't promise anything."

"Is Erick why you need to go talk to Kylie right now?"

"Yes. I'll explain when I get back, but right now, I need to talk to her."

Tom turned to Emily. "I have to go out, Emily. You're going to stay with my mom and the dogs for a little while, okay?"

Tears welled up in Emily's eyes as she looked at him. "You're leaving, too?"

He shook his head and sat beside her on the bed, pulling her into his arms for a hug. "No. Not at all. I just have to run a quick errand. I'll be back right away. I promise."

"What if you don't come back?"

"You don't have to worry because I will. I just need to go talk to one of my friends." He glanced at his watch then took it off and put it on her tiny wrist. "Here. When this little hand is on the three, I'll be back. Okay?" He had four hours to get to Kylie's house, talk to her, and get back to Emily. Plenty of time.

"Promise?"

He nodded, hugged her again, and kissed the top of her head. "I promise, and I bet my mom will help you find a book to read with the dogs. Maybe you guys can even find something good to watch on TV."

Hazel appeared in the doorway. "I have some princess movies upstairs. Will you watch *Snow White* with me, Emily? It's been my favorite story for a really long time."

"I like Snow White. The dwarfs are funny."

"Which one is your favorite?" Hazel asked as she led Emily to the living room. The dogs followed happily, and Tom smiled, thankful for his mother's willingness to help.

Emily didn't even seem to notice when he put his coat on and left.

Chapter 23

KYLIE WAS EATING a bowl of frosted cereal for lunch when someone knocked on her kitchen door. When she saw it was Tom, she let him in and returned to the table. "What's up?"

"I'm not sure how to tell you."

"Tell me what?"

"My investigator thinks he found Erick."

Kylie's throat closed up. She'd hoped it would never happen. That way, she would never have to decide if she was serious about not wanting to meet him. "And?"

"The boy is in a foster home. His adoptive parents died a year ago."

"How?"

"In a car accident."

Kylie set her spoon down and pushed the bowl away. "I feel sick."

"I thought you should know. You told me you wanted to find him too."

"I do. I just don't know what I want to do about it now that he's been found. If he's been found." She didn't know what she would do if Erick was different than she'd imagined. Or how would she react if she put herself out there, only to be rejected by the boy she gave birth to? She didn't know if she could live with his rejection. On the other end of the spectrum, she had absolutely no idea what she would do if Erick wanted her in his life. If he was the boy in foster care, she wanted him more than anything, but she was realistic enough to know that things probably wouldn't just be as simple as walking in and saying, "Hey, I'm your mom. Why don't you come live with me?"

"If it's our son, I want him. I'll fight for custody." Tom grinned. "Actually, it doesn't sound like there would be much fighting. If he's in foster care, returning him to his biological parents should be pretty easy. The investigator has the results back from the DNA test."

She felt like the blood in her body stopped moving, and she shivered. "He already did the test?"

"Yeah. That was the next step, and we submitted our samples right after you agreed to look for him with me. Why wouldn't he run the test?"

"I figured he'd let us know when Erick was found and then do the test when we were ready." She wasn't sure she would ever be ready. *Don't get your hopes up. It's not Erick.*

"We are ready. Haven't you been waiting for this ever since you learned Erick was alive?"

She wanted to scream, "No! I never wanted this." But she couldn't. With just a little bit of luck, everything would be fine. Fate certainly owed her that little bit of luck. "Okay."

"Are you sure you're okay?"

"Yes, I just need a little time to adjust." Her world was spinning on its axis, and she didn't have anyone to talk to about it. She couldn't even voice her worries to herself, but the DNA test might force her to face the past.

"We're supposed to meet with him in the morning."

"Who?" *Please not the boy. I'm not ready to see him.*

"The investigator. Who else?" He narrowed his eyes at her. "Are you sure you're okay?"

* * *

Kylie slid her hand over the cool conference table, fighting the urge to clench her fists in her lap. She'd sat up in the kitchen all night. She had realized on the drive to the office that she was wearing the same jeans and sweatshirt she'd worn the previous day, and now they were waiting for the investigator. Leaning toward Tom, she whispered, "What is taking so long?"

"I don't know."

"Well, we're here, and he's late. It's rude."

"You're just nervous. Calm down."

Kylie glared at him, furious that he was telling her to calm down. He had no idea the turmoil she was going through, and she was about to tell him off when the door to the conference room opened. A short, round man, who would only need a fake beard and a wig to play Santa, walked in.

When he introduced himself, Kylie jumped at the sound of his squeaky voice. He sounded like a mouse who liked to suck helium from balloons. Kylie shook his outstretched hand then wiped her hand on her pants, disgusted by the cold, clammy feel of his skin.

After greeting Tom, the investigator lowered himself into a chair and cleared his throat as he flipped open a folder. "I had you two come in today so we could discuss a couple things. I have some good news and some bad news."

Kylie clenched her fists and focused on her fingernails digging into her palms. She hadn't expected Erick to be found so easily, and now she held her breath.

The investigator looked at Kylie over the top of his gold-rimmed reading glasses. "Miss Killian, the DNA test reveals the boy I found in foster care is your son."

She swallowed repeatedly. She'd been telling herself all along that this boy wasn't her son. Now that she knew he was, she realized how badly she wanted to meet him, to hug him, to whisk him away and never let him go.

Tom beamed at Kylie and reached for her hand. "We found our son."

Kylie let him take her hand as she stared at the table. Even though she wanted to meet Erick, she knew she didn't want to force Erick into any sort of relationship. All she could do was hope she would be able to convince Tom to let Erick make up his own mind instead of pushing for custody right away.

"What do we do now?" Tom asked. "Can we meet him? I don't think he should remain in foster care. I mean, we never gave him up. We have rights, don't we?"

So much for Tom taking things slow.

"Well…" The investigator looked back at his paper. "Here's the bad news, Tom."

She swallowed and looked up from the table to see the investigator still peering at her. He cleared his throat, took a drink of water, then finally spoke. "The boy's DNA doesn't match yours, Tom."

Kylie pulled her hand from Tom's, rose from the table, sickened. She couldn't imagine what Tom's reaction was going to be once he understood, but she knew she had to find a restroom.

"What?" Tom asked.

"The DNA test says that you're not the father—"

Kylie let the door slam behind her as she ran down the hall to the exit. She had to get away from the room, away from the investigator, and away from Tom. Not knowing where to find a restroom in the building, she rushed out to the street, wishing she'd never agreed to ride with Tom. If she'd driven, she would be able to escape without having to talk to anyone.

She made it to the edge of the sidewalk before she doubled over and vomited in the gutter. As her stomach released its contents, her eyes welled up with tears. She couldn't stop either action, and she began sobbing.

She'd just straightened up and was searching for a tissue in her purse when Tom walked out of the building and glared at her. "You told me all along it was mine. I've been torn up about this for eleven years, and you were sleeping with someone other than me."

She shook her head. "It wasn't like that, Tom," she whispered. "I swear."

"What? You thought you'd just claim it was my baby so you could get the Mallock name and money? Who's the father? Some lowlife piece of shit, I'm sure."

Kylie finally dug a tissue from her purse and wiped her face. "Let me explain." It was the last thing in the world she wanted to talk about, but she knew she owed him an explanation.

"I don't want to hear any more of your lies." He turned on his heel and stalked to his truck. Without a look back, he left her on the sidewalk.

She was still standing there when a Jeep stopped next to her. "Kylie? Are you okay?"

Kylie turned from where she had watched Tom's truck squeal out of the parking lot. She couldn't meet his eyes, but she knew it was Lance from his concerned voice. "No, I'm not. I need a ride home."

"Sure, come on." He reached across the seat and opened the door.

She got in, buckled her seat belt, and wiped at her eyes again. "Thanks."

"What's going on?"

Her body shook as she tried to control her sobs. "We just

met with Tom's investigator. Erick has been found."

"Why the tears?"

"He's not Tom's son."

Lance turned in his seat, slack-jawed as he stared at her. "What?"

She shook her head. "I thought he was Tom's." She clenched her hands together. "I hoped he was Tom's."

"What's going on, Kylie? Tell me what's going on."

Instead of telling him the truth, she shook her head. Tom was the only one who needed to know the truth. "Never mind. I'm not going to defend myself. No one is going to believe me, anyway. Can you just take me home?"

Lance pressed his lips together and nodded. "Yeah."

On the drive to Kylie's house, they were silent. She suspected he was furious with her, thinking she'd lied all along about the baby and thinking that she was the kind of girl who willingly slept with someone other than Tom when she was fifteen.

Kylie knew all she had to do was tell Lance the truth about the baby, but she couldn't. She'd never told anyone she'd been raped. Not even Mira knew. Kylie had always hoped the baby was Tom's. She could handle knowing that Tom had a kid out there somewhere. She couldn't handle knowing that her son was fathered by her rapist.

By the time Lance pulled up to Kylie's house, she knew what she had to do. "Thanks for the ride. I'm sorry for everything," she said as she opened the door and got out. Before he could respond, she slammed the door and ran up to the house.

Once inside, she went straight to her closet and pulled out her suitcase. Mira's wedding was in six days, and as soon as her best friend and her cousin were married, Kylie was leaving Chinkapin—for good, this time. There wasn't anything that would bring her back. There wasn't anything that could fix knowing she'd given birth to Vernon Tallbaum's baby.

Chapter 24

WHEN TOM'S CELL phone rang an hour after he left his investigator's office, he picked it up and was surprised to see Lance's number. "Hey, what's up?"

"What the hell is going on with Kylie?"

Tom forced himself to ignore the initial flicker of worry and reminded himself Kylie had cheated on him and lied about it for eleven years. "No idea. Why?"

"You need to talk to her."

"I don't have to do anything. I'm not sure how you found out, but she cheated on me."

"I know. I just gave her a ride home since you left her in town."

"Like you would have given her a ride home after she did that to you?" Tom poured himself a glass of Scotch, only one until Emily fell asleep. "If you want to help me, why don't you help me find Eva?"

"She's still not back?" Lance asked.

"No."

"What happened?"

"She just disappeared. She left me a note saying she'd be back as soon as possible. She left her phone on the nightstand. I called everyone whose number is in her phone. No one knows where she is, or at least no one is telling me where she is."

"I'll look into it."

"I hope you have better luck than my investigator is."

"All right. I'll check into it, but only if you agree to talk to Kylie."

Tom closed his eyes and frowned. He needed to find Eva for Emily. He didn't need to talk to Kylie for any reason, but Lance never said how soon he had to talk to Kylie. "Fine."

Forty-five minutes later, Lance called back.

"Did you find her?" Tom asked in lieu of greeting his

brother.

"Yeah. She's in jail."

Tom muted the television. "What? No. That can't be right. Why?"

"This report says she turned herself in for a drunk driving charge."

Tom punched the couch cushion beside him, causing Emily to look up from where she was combing the dog's hair. "When?"

"Three days ago."

"She was driving drunk three days ago?" Eva wouldn't drink while she was pregnant. At least Tom didn't think so, but he realized that he knew very little about her.

"No. It's an old charge. For whatever reason, she turned herself in. Looks like it was in Beltrami county."

"Beltrami? Isn't that Bemidji?"

"Yeah."

"Thank God."

"Why are you so worried? You've disappeared before."

Tom pinched the bridge of his nose. "I'm not pregnant, though, and I didn't leave my kid—not that I have one—at someone's house with zero warning or explanation."

"What?"

Tom sighed and rose from the couch. He hadn't meant to reveal anything to Lance, but he couldn't avoid it now. He wasn't going to discuss it in front of Emily, though. "She's pregnant. That's why she came to my house, and yes, this baby is mine."

"You never learn, do you?"

"Apparently, I have super sperm. Eva had an IUD. We're not sure why it didn't work. I've barely talked to her since I found out."

"You're unbelievable."

Tom chuckled even though he didn't see anything humorous about his baby's mother being in jail. "I sense that you don't mean that in a good way. How long is she going to be in jail?"

"I have no idea what's going on. You need to talk to her. I can give you a number to call and talk to someone, but Eva gets to decide who visits her while she's in there."

"Fine. Give me the number."

After Tom wrote down the number, he said, "Hey, about what you saw with Kylie and me. It was just a kiss, and it was my fault. I knew she was drunk and missing you. She was lonely, and I thought if I kissed her, I might have a better chance convincing her to seek custody of Erick with me, but Erick's not mine, so there's no need to mess around with Kylie."

"You were using Kylie just to get to Erick?"

Tom swallowed. "Yeah," he muttered. It was better for Lance to think he was a complete asshole than for him to know how completely in love he had been with Kylie and how devastated he was to learn she'd been unfaithful.

"What are you doing with Eva and the baby?"

"I don't know, Lance. You should know by now that I never have the right answers. I'm still figuring shit out, but I do know that I'm not interested in Kylie." Maybe Lance and Kylie could be together now that it was clear Kylie wasn't who Tom had been in love with for years. "She loves you."

"Okay."

"Okay, we're cool, and you're not mad at Kylie anymore?"

"No. Okay as in thanks for telling me."

Tom turned to look out the window and spotted a squirrel running across the snow, which reminded him of snowshoeing with Kylie. Everything reminded him of Kylie. It had been that way for twelve years; it was ridiculous to think his brain would stop thinking of her now just because he'd learned the truth about her. "So you're still pissed at Kylie?"

"I have to get to work. I don't have time to discuss this with you right now."

"Want to get together for a beer after work? I can probably convince Mom to watch Emily for a bit."

"Maybe. It depends on how my day goes."

"Fair enough. Thanks again for letting me know about Eva." Tom ended the call and stared out the window. He had no idea that Eva had outstanding drunk driving charges. She was always the designated driver for him when they'd gone out. The only time he'd even seen her have more than a few drinks was when they were home in Montana. He couldn't imagine why she'd decided to turn herself in now. He dialed the number Lance had given him.

Fifteen minutes later, he hung up in frustration. They couldn't connect him to Eva, but they let him leave a message for her. Since he wasn't on her list of allowed visitors, all he could do was wait until she called or was released and came back for Emily. They wouldn't even tell him when she was going to be released. Her sentence was for ninety days. The only useful information he'd received was that normally, well-behaved prisoners were released early.

* * *

Five days later, shortly after Tom tucked Emily into bed, someone knocked on Tom's door. He opened it and glared at Eva. "Where have you been?"

Eva hunched her shoulders against the wind. "You know where I was."

"Fine. Why in the world wouldn't you talk to me while you were there? You just leave your daughter with me and won't talk to me?" He backed up to let her in. Even though he was angry with her, he wasn't going to keep her from Emily.

"I knew she'd be safe here, and I didn't want to talk to you because I had to figure some stuff out for myself."

Tom felt his heart stop. "What kind of stuff?" Please don't say you decided to have an abortion.

"What to do about the baby."

Tom believed it was her right to choose what to do with her body, but he hoped that she would at least consider his opinion before making any decisions. He swallowed and tried to speak in a normal voice. "And what did you decide?"

"That we need to talk."

Tom's shoulders relaxed as he let out the breath he held. "I agree. How about now?"

Eva stepped forward and kissed his cheek. "Actually, I know you're not going to believe this, but I'd really like to see Emily. I didn't realize how much I'd miss her."

"She's in bed. I tucked her in at eight." He glanced at his watch. 8:43. "Hopefully, she's asleep by now."

"That's fine. I'm not going to wake her up. I just want to see her."

"Okay." He sat on the couch as Eva walked down the hall

to Emily's room.

When Eva returned ten minutes later, she sat on the other end of the sofa. "Thank you for taking care of her."

He nodded. "It would have been nice to have a little warning, though."

"I was afraid you'd say 'no' if I gave you the opportunity."

"Yet you left her here?"

"I trust you, Tom. You're a good guy, and I knew you wouldn't blame her for my mistakes."

"She's a little kid. Nothing is her fault."

Eva tucked her feet beneath her on the couch. "What do you think we should do about the baby?"

"Have it, raise it, and spoil it." Tom wasn't sure of much in his life, but he was certain of what he wanted to do with the baby. No matter how irresponsible Eva was, the baby hadn't done anything wrong, and it deserved to have everything he could—and would—provide.

"What about Erick? And Kylie?"

Tom tipped his head to the side, cracking his neck. "They're not my concern anymore."

"What? Why not?"

"He's not my kid." Eva was the first person he'd told. He felt as if his heart was breaking. He'd loved a child for eleven years only to find out that child wasn't his and the woman he'd loved was a liar who'd slept with someone else while they were dating. His love had been one-sided and a complete sham. "My investigator found Kylie's son. He's not mine."

Eva stared at him, open-mouthed, for a few seconds. "How can that be?"

"Obviously, she was screwing around with some loser and thought it would be better to claim the kid was mine. Think about it. If you were screwing two guys and got pregnant, wouldn't you claim the father was the one with more money?"

She scratched the side of her neck. "I admit I don't really know her, but that doesn't sound like something Kylie would do."

"Before I found out, I never would have believed it of her either. I guess she fooled all of us."

They were both silent for a few minutes, until Tom shook off his anger at Kylie. "So, as I said, they're not my concern anymore. They don't affect me."

"I think they still do. You're not the kind of guy to give up on someone you've loved for so long."

"I loved a lie. Two lies. It's over now."

Eva gave a curt nod. "Okay. If you say it's over, then it's over."

He wasn't sure he believed she would let it go that easily, but at least they were done talking about it for now. "You asked what I thought we should do."

"I did."

"Let's get married. I can take care of you, Emily, and the baby. We can be a family." If he couldn't have Kylie and Erick, then Eva, Emily, and their baby were the next best things.

"We don't have to get married to be a family." Eva took his hand and pulled him closer. "Besides, I'm not a big fan of marriage."

"Why?"

"I've been married. I didn't see anything special about it." Her laughter lightened his mood. "Besides, what if we get tired of each other. If we're married, we have to take all those legal steps to become unmarried. Those are a pain in the ass."

"Are they?"

She nodded. "Not to mention the pain in the ass of getting married. Let's just stay friends."

Tom frowned before speaking. "Friends raising a couple kids together?" He hadn't acted as though he was in love with her, but he thought proposing would make it clear he was serious about taking care of her and the baby.

"Sure. Why not?" She smiled at him. "Besides, Emily's been through a lot already. I don't think we should rush into anything."

Tom couldn't argue with her putting Emily first. "What was Emily's dad like?"

"He was a great guy. I'm sure she'll miss him more than she'd ever miss me. He worshipped her and spent as much of his time with her as he could." Eva stared at the fireplace.

"Sounds nice. Poor Emily."

"Yeah. I feel bad for her. Now she's pretty much living with strangers."

"I think she's adjusting well. I'm sure she'll be happy to see you. Tomorrow, we should go buy some furniture for her room."

"Her room? Furniture?"

"Sure. If you guys are staying here for a while, she should have her own room and furniture she likes. Not bachelor furniture."

"I didn't say we were staying."

Tom wasn't going to let Eva leave. She was carrying his baby, and he'd already gone through the agony of wondering where his kid was. "I know. I want you guys to stay, though. If you're not willing to marry me, even though I promise it won't be like your previous marriage, I still want you guys to live here and let me take care of you."

"How are you going to take care of us? You don't even have a job."

"I'll go back to the plant." He tapped his fingers on the arm of the couch. "I need to do something. I'm tired of just sitting around waiting for Kylie to—" Realizing he'd almost said "love me," he coughed a couple of times. "Waiting for Kylie to agree to help find Erick."

Eva narrowed her eyes, and he knew she had a pretty good idea of what he'd been about to say. "Just like that?"

"I've been talking to my mom and dad again, and it's not like they stole my son. I told Mom I'd work harder at forgiving them."

"I can't marry someone who drinks as much as you."

"Me? I'm not the one who had a DUI charge." Tom crossed his arms angrily. "And if you're so worried about my drinking, why the hell did you leave your daughter here with me?"

"I didn't have any other options."

"And what are your options now? When you want to run off and party, who is going to watch your kid for you? Kids, I mean. You think you can just show up on my doorstep, hand me my baby and Emily, and take off whenever you want, conveniently forgetting my drinking problem because you need a babysitter? It's not going to work that way."

Eva sighed. "I'll think about it."

"You don't sound very excited about it."

"There was a time when I would have leapt at the chance to

be Mrs. Tom Mallock, but right now, I feel like you proposed for all the wrong reasons."

"I proposed because you're pregnant with my child." He raised an eyebrow. "It is mine, right?"

She rose to pace in front of the fireplace. "Of course. As soon as we can, we'll have a paternity test done to calm your nerves about that, but we don't have to get married just because we're going to have a baby." She ran her hands through her short hair. "If I get married again, it's going to be because I'm in love."

"You don't love me?" Tom had been certain she did. Kylie had said that Eva must love him, but then again, Kylie had been known to lie.

Eva blanched, but she nodded. "Of course I do, but I want my husband to love me too."

He stared into the fire. "I love you." Or at least he loved the idea of having a family and his own child.

"You've been in love with Kylie forever. Now you're mad at her. That doesn't mean you love me."

"I'm a rotten person, and yes, I hoped to have a family with Kylie and Erick because I felt I owed them that. Now I realize I was just using them as an excuse to keep you at a distance."

"I'm not surprised, and that's why I don't want to get married."

"Ever?"

She kissed his cheek. "I don't know. Maybe someday, I'll know without a doubt that you love me and don't feel obligated to be with me because I got pregnant, but for now, my answer has to be no."

"I can understand that. Does that mean you'll stay, though?" He didn't know how to convince her to stay. "I really want you guys to stay. I want to make some stuff up to you."

"What stuff?"

"You deserve more than me treating you like you were just a friend with benefits." He rubbed the back of his neck. "I deserve more than waiting around for Kylie to come to her senses. Thank God I found out the truth before—"

"Yes, we'll stay for a while."

"Excellent." He grinned and squeezed her hand. "Are you busy tomorrow?"

"I just want to spend the day with Emily. Why?"

"There's this wedding tomorrow. I was wondering if you'd like to be my second date for it."

"Second date?"

"Yeah. Emily was going to be my date. I'm afraid she'll change her mind when she realizes you're back, so I thought you should go with us. Keefe told me that it's fine if I bring someone."

"Whose wedding?"

"Keefe and Mira's." Tom swallowed. "Mira is Kylie's best friend. She was my personal assistant at the plant. Keefe is Kylie's cousin."

"Well, that's a little awkward, isn't it?"

"Not really. I'm not going to do anything to make things uncomfortable for Keefe and Mira. I'll just avoid Kylie." He tried to ignore the yawning pit of emptiness in his stomach when he thought of walking down the aisle with Kylie on his arm.

Chapter 25

KYLIE SWALLOWED DEEPLY and walked up to Tom and Lance at the front of the church. It was February fourteenth, and she hadn't spoken to either of the Mallock brothers since the day she'd met with Tom's investigator. Whether Tom wanted to or not, he was going to have to be polite to her since Mira and Keefe were getting married in two hours. "Hey," she said.

Tom turned from Lance, looked her up and down, then nodded at her. "Hey."

She fought the urge to retreat. "Can we talk?"

"We don't have anything to talk about."

"Come on, man," Lance said. "Give her a chance to explain."

"I don't know how she can possibly explain what she did."

"You're right. There's no explanation or excuse for what I did. I don't expect you to forgive me or ever understand." She swallowed nervously. "Actually, I don't expect you to ever listen to me try to explain it. I just don't want to screw up Mira's wedding. So if you could just pretend not to want me dead for today, that'd be awesome."

Tom frowned then nodded. "Fair enough."

"Thanks." She turned to walk away.

Lance grabbed her arm. "Kylie."

Kylie met his gaze evenly. "I have to go help Mira get ready."

When he released her arm, she turned and walked away.

* * *

Kylie stood with her back against the wall at Keefe and Mira's wedding reception. The wedding had been beautiful. She'd managed to walk down the aisle with Tom, and they'd been polite to one another the entire evening. At the moment, Tom was dancing with Emily as Eva watched from the sidelines.

Eva's approach startled Kylie, who fumbled for a few seconds before she spoke. "I love your dress. It's great."

Eva smoothed her hands over the turquoise fabric at her hips. "Thanks. I'm glad I was able to find something at the last minute."

"Yeah. Shopping around here can be hit or miss."

Eva tipped her head to the side. "Can I ask you a question?"

Kylie took a deep breath and closed her eyes for a second, steeling herself. She didn't know what Tom had told Eva, or what Eva would want to ask her. When she opened her eyes, she nodded. "Yeah. What's up?"

"What's with you and Tom?"

"Nothing. Didn't he tell you?" Kylie tucked a tendril of hair that had escaped her updo behind her ear, wishing she felt as comfortable as Eva seemed to.

"What happened? Why didn't you know Erick wasn't his?"

"It doesn't matter, does it? Tom isn't his father, and I didn't tell him the truth."

"I don't think you'd lie about that. If you were that kind of person, Tom wouldn't have been in love with you all this time."

Baring her soul wasn't Kylie's plan for the night. Even if it was, Eva wouldn't be her chosen confidant. "Why are you asking me, Eva? I have nothing to do with Tom."

Eva took a sip from the punch glass she held. "Yeah, I just wanted to hear it from you. I love Tom."

"Then I wish you all the best." They both watched Tom spinning a giggling Emily for a moment. "He really likes your daughter," Kylie said. "I think he really likes you. Maybe now that he's over me, he'll realize how great you are."

"You think I'm great? You don't even know me."

"You took care of Tom when he needed you. It's clear that you love him, which can't be easy when he's been obsessed with finding Erick."

Eva smiled and patted Kylie's arm. "I don't know what happened, and I'm sorry for any pain it's causing you, but I'm so glad he's decided he doesn't love you anymore."

Ignoring the stab of pain at hearing Tom didn't love her anymore, Kylie smiled and nodded. "Believe it or not, I'm glad too."

"Are you going to get back with Lance?"

Kylie shook her head. "No. Our relationship was great until we came back here. Here is where Lance wants to be. I've learned my lesson about trying to relive the past."

"I'm not sure Lance agrees."

"What do you mean?" It was ridiculous to think she and Lance could make it work. They had even more issues than before, and she still didn't want to be in Chinkapin.

Eva gestured toward the bridal party table where Lance sat, staring at the two of them. When Kylie's eyes met his, the left side of his mouth curled up in a smile.

Kylie couldn't tear her eyes from him as he rose and walked toward her. His broad shoulders filled out the dark-gray suit perfectly, and he'd had his hair trimmed for the wedding. When he was directly in front of her, he held out his hand. "Dance?"

Kylie sighed and nodded. A dance couldn't hurt anything. She still planned on leaving in the morning. She placed her hand in his and followed him onto the dance floor. She wasn't sure why he was being nice to her again. Maybe he figured that Tom and Eva were together, giving him a clear shot at reconciling with Kylie.

They arranged themselves in a clandestine dance pose and swayed to the music. "I see Eva's back," Lance said.

"Yep."

"How's that working out with you and Tom?"

She brushed her fingers over his shoulder to remove a small piece of lint from his suit jacket. "I'm not seeing Tom. You know that."

He leaned back slightly and shook his head. "I meant with clearing up the Erick issue."

Kylie met his gaze quickly then turned her attention to the clock on the wall behind him. Telling Tom the truth would be more painful than letting him believe she'd cheated on him. Besides, Eva was pregnant with Tom's baby. He was supposed to be with her instead. "Tom can believe what he wants to believe. I'm not going to argue with him. He has a right to his opinion."

"Even if his opinion isn't based on the truth?"

"What makes you think he doesn't know the truth?"

Unwilling to discuss the issue further, she tried to pull away from him, but he held tight.

"Because it's you, Kylie. You're not like that."

"What makes you so sure? I kissed Tom, didn't I?"

"Kissing isn't the same as lying about fathering a child. You need to talk to him."

"What is it you think I should tell him?"

"The truth. I can't believe you purposely lied to him. Talk to him and clear this up."

"No." She pressed her cheek against his shoulder so he couldn't see the tears welling up in her eyes then jerked away from him when her tears overwhelmed her. "It's over and done."

"Come on, Kylie. Wait."

"No, I can't do this. I won't do this." She turned and rushed to the restroom. After locking herself in a stall, she pressed the heels of her hands to her eyes. She wasn't about to discuss being raped with Lance. She certainly wasn't going to tell Tom about it. He could—and would—believe whatever he wanted about her.

The tap of high heels entering the bathroom warned her she wasn't alone, so she took a deep breath then dabbed at her eyes with a tissue, hoping her tears hadn't ruined her makeup. As she reached for the lock on the stall door, a cell phone rang.

"Hey. I was wondering when you'd call me. I've missed you," Eva said.

Kylie froze, curious who Eva had missed.

"Yeah, you heard right. I was in jail for a drunk driving charge, but I'm out now."

Kylie reached to open the stall door again.

"I'm living with Tom. He proposed when I told him I was pregnant."

Kylie slumped against the wall. Tom had proposed to Eva. He hadn't even listened to her explanation; he'd just moved on.

"Oh, hell no. I'm not pregnant. I was just trying to get him to pay attention to me. You know, he's been hung up on that chick he screwed in high school forever."

Kylie straightened up and pulled her own cell phone from her tiny clutch. She tapped the screen to bring up the voice recorder, hoping Eva would have more to say about lying to

Tom.

She didn't disappoint. "I can't get pregnant. I had my tubes removed when I had Emily. I'm not making that mistake again. I'll accept his proposal tonight, and a couple weeks after our rushed wedding, I'll have a miscarriage."

After a few seconds of silence, Eva continued. "Look, I have to go. I'll talk to you in a few days. Everything will work out."

Kylie ended the recorder on her phone and waited until she heard the squeak of the bathroom door before she left the stall.

She fixed her makeup the best she could and straightened her shoulders. Even if Tom hated her, he deserved to know what Eva was up to.

As she walked back into the reception room, Kylie scanned the crowd, looking for Tom. He and Eva were dancing, but as Kylie watched, she noticed that Tom kept looking toward her. When he noticed she was staring at him, he glowered across the room and guided Eva to the other side of the dance floor.

When the music ended, Kylie stepped onto the floor and wove through the crowd to where she'd last seen Tom and Eva. The two of them had made their way to a small table near the bridal party's.

Eva noticed Kylie first and smiled up at her. "Hi, Kylie. Are you having a good time?"

Kylie shook her head. "Not really. Especially since I just came from the bathroom."

"Are you okay?" Tom asked then quickly looked at Eva. "I mean, who cares if you're having a good time."

Eva's face paled as Kylie stared at her.

"I think Eva has something to tell you about her pregnancy."

"Not now," Eva said.

"Why not?" Kylie asked and leaned down. "Actually, you're right. You probably don't want to do this here. We can go outside."

"I'm not going anywhere with you, Kylie," Tom said.

Lance approached the table. "Hey, are you going to finish that dance with me?" he asked Kylie.

"Not right now. I need to talk to Tom." She narrowed her

eyes. "Or Eva does."

Lance glanced around at the small group. "What's going on?"

Kylie looked pointedly at Eva. Lance turned his attention to Eva. Tom shifted his gaze to her as well and sighed. "What's she talking about, Eva?"

"I don't know." Eva smiled sweetly. "Don't you want another drink? Let's go get another drink from the bar."

Tom glared at Kylie and nodded. "Yeah, let's do that. I don't like the company here."

Kylie grabbed his hand. "Tom, wait."

"Kylie, let it go," Lance said, reaching for her.

"Leave me alone, Lance." She gripped Tom's hand and tried to ignore how his hand stayed perfectly limp in hers. "She's not pregnant."

"How would you know?"

Eva slid her arm around Tom's waist. "She's lying just because she doesn't want you to be happy, Tom."

"I'm not lying, Tom. Listen to me."

"No, thanks. I don't really believe anything you have to say anymore." He shook her hand off his and turned to Eva. "Should we get out of here?"

"Fine. If you don't believe anything I say, what about what Eva has to say? Do you believe her word?"

Tom turned back and leaned close to whisper angrily. "I don't know what you're up to, but you're making a scene at your cousin and best friend's wedding reception. It's not very flattering."

"And you're making a mistake." She held up her phone and pressed the button that played the recording.

"I can't get pregnant. I had my tubes removed when I had Emily. I'm not making that mistake again. I'll accept his proposal tonight, and a couple weeks after our rushed wedding, I'll have a miscarriage." The recording wasn't great, but it was clearly Eva's voice.

Tom's gaze shifted from the recorder to Eva. "Is it true?"

"Of course not. I was just joking with a friend on the phone."

"Bullshit." He turned to Kylie. "And haven't you fucked up my life enough already? Just leave me alone."

Kylie blinked, and her hand fell to her side. "I just wanted you to know."

"Sure you did. Because if I'm not with Eva, you can convince yourself I'm in love with you still. But it turns out that you're not the only one who lied, Kylie. I never loved you. It was a dare. Someone dared me to sleep with you in high school. I didn't give a damn about you, but I wasn't about to let my baby suffer because I was a foolish kid."

Kylie drew her lower lip between her teeth and nodded. "Fair enough." She refused to let her heart break in public. She turned from Tom, trying to ignore the crowd of people who stared at the small group in the corner. She made her way to the coat room and slid her arms into her jacket.

Lance touched her arm. "You okay?"

"Fine. Why wouldn't I be?"

"Because my brother just claimed he never loved you."

She took a deep breath. "I already told you that we're over and done with. It doesn't matter what Tom thinks of me."

"What about me?"

"That's over and done too," she whispered.

He moved his hand from her waist and cupped her cheek, turning her face toward his. "It doesn't have to be. I still love you."

She blinked rapidly, trying to make her tears disappear, but they seeped out of her eyes.

"I love you," he repeated as he wiped the tears with his thumbs. He stared into her eyes as he bowed his head and kissed her gently. "Do you still love me?"

She nodded once then wrapped her arms tightly around his neck and kissed him. His mouth on hers was warm and made her sigh with happiness, but it didn't light a fire in her soul. "So much," she whispered when she pulled away.

"Then it's not over. Even if you never tell me what happened, I know you're not the person Tom is pretending to believe you are."

His unwavering faith in her made her smile. When she was in his arms, she forgot the bad parts of her life. "I miss you."

"I miss you too."

"Do you want to get out of here?" she asked.

"Yeah. Where do you want to go?"

"My place?" There was nothing she could do to convince Tom they should be together, but she could have one last night with Lance before she left town.

"I thought you'd never ask." After grabbing his coat, they rushed outside to his Jeep. As she closed her door and Lance rounded the front of the Jeep, she saw Tom, Eva, and Emily getting into his truck. They didn't appear to be happily in love.

Lance settled into the driver's seat and started the Jeep.

Instead of thinking about Lance's kiss and their upcoming sex, Kylie was focused on the red Ford truck parked across the lot. Even though she suspected she could forget about Tom for a little while if she took Lance home with her, she knew it was the wrong thing to do.

"Lance, we can't do this."

"Sure we can. You just said that it's over and done with Tom."

She nodded. "I did, and I do love you, but I'm not in love with you. If we go to my house, it doesn't change anything. We weren't happy together. You don't trust me. You don't accept that you're partly to blame for our problems."

"I'll work on it. We can fix it if we keep trying."

Kylie shook her head. "As much as I wish I loved you like you love me, and as much as I want to believe we can be happy together, it just doesn't seem realistic to me."

Lance sighed and rubbed his hands over his face. "Why did you kiss me, then?"

"Because my heart was broken." She looked down at her hands and took a deep breath. "I love you because you care about me, and I wish that I loved you enough to make it work, but you're right. I am still in love with Tom. You weren't right not to trust me, because I never did anything with him while you and I were together."

She reached for the door handle. "I'm sorry for hurting you. I'm sorry for not telling you the truth, but now I have."

He stared straight ahead. "You should go."

"Yes, I should."

Chapter 26

TOM FOLLOWED EVA and Emily into his house. "Is it true?" he asked, unable to wait any longer. He didn't want to believe Kylie. He wanted a life that was easy and completely honest.

Eva narrowed her eyes. "You believe her? You actually have to ask me what the truth is when she lied to you for years about being the father of her kid?"

"I notice you're not answering the question."

"Of course I'm not answering the question. I don't think it's worth being answered." She looked pointedly at Emily. "Go get ready for bed."

"Why are you guys arguing?" Emily asked with a big yawn.

"We're not arguing." Tom forced himself to take a deep breath and relax. "We just need to discuss some stuff after you go to bed, okay?"

"What kind of stuff?"

Eva pointed down the hallway. "Emily. Bed. Now."

Emily looked at Tom with a quivering lower lip then turned to go to bed.

He couldn't stand to see the little girl so upset. "Get changed into your pajamas, and I'll be in to read you a story in a few minutes, okay?"

Emily nodded and kept walking.

"Why are you so mean to her?" Tom asked quietly. "She's just a little kid. It's not her fault that I'm questioning you."

"No, of course it's not her fault. It's that lying bitch's fault."

"She's not a"—Tom blew out a deep breath—"lying bitch. I just want to know what the hell is going on."

"Fine." Eva spun to look at him. "Why don't you pour yourself a big glass of Scotch then read a story to Emily? By the time you're done spoiling her, maybe I'll be ready to talk."

"Maybe," Tom muttered. He hung up his coat and went into the kitchen to pour himself a glass of Scotch, not that he needed it to deal with Emily. He just needed to calm himself down a little before talking with Eva.

For whatever reason, she hadn't just come right out and denied lying about being pregnant, maybe because she didn't think he would believe her after hearing her voice on Kylie's phone.

After reading Emily a story, he returned to the living room. Eva waited on the couch, reading a magazine.

He was unable to control his anger any longer. "Are you pregnant?"

Eva slowly raised her gaze to his. "No."

He clenched his jaw. "Were you pregnant?"

She shook her head.

He pointed at the door. "Get the fuck out."

"What? You're throwing me out? What's the big deal?"

"You lied to me. You knew exactly what would hurt me the most, and you used it to get what you wanted."

"That's not true." She stood and threw her magazine at him. "I love you, dammit. You have no interest in anything other than Kylie and Erick. I thought maybe, just maybe, that if you thought I was pregnant, you'd start thinking of someone other than her. Maybe you'd realize that you loved me."

He kicked the magazine out of his way as he strode to the kitchen. After pouring another glass of Scotch, he turned to her. "We're through. You are going to pack your shit and get the hell out of here."

"What about Emily? You expect me to wake her up and leave with her tonight?"

"You don't give a shit about her." He swallowed and saw Emily's quivering lip in his head. "In the morning, you're going to explain to Emily that you guys are leaving. You're going to treat that girl the way she deserves to be treated for the rest of her life. You're not going to dump her with strangers and disappear for weeks or months at a time."

"You can't tell me what to do."

"Don't push me, Eva. You don't know what kind of person I am or can be. Just trust me that you don't want to harm Emily in any way."

"I can't believe you're upset about this. How is this worse than what Kylie did to you?"

"I never said it was." He spread his arms and turned in a

circle slowly. "She's not here either, is she?"

"I doubt it'll be that way for long," Eva snarled and stormed from the room to slam the guest room door.

Tom sank onto the couch and stared at the fire as he wondered how accurate Eva was. He already missed Kylie and regretted the way he'd reacted to learning Erick wasn't his son.

Chapter 27

KYLIE TOOK A deep breath and opened the door to the county's social services office. She didn't expect to accomplish much by meeting Erick, but she would feel better if she could just assure herself he'd turned out better than he would have if she'd raised him.

Once she was in the conference room she'd been directed to, she couldn't decide whether to sit or stand as she looked out the window. She didn't want to appear too eager to meet him because she didn't want to give him any indication that she wanted to spend the rest of her life with him. She missed him. She'd fantasized about him being alive and with her. But she refused to push him into something he didn't want.

"Miss Killian, I'm so glad you were able to make it in today." A short woman with long black hair smiled at her from the doorway. "I'm Christina." When she stepped to the side, Kylie's knees buckled at the sight of the boy behind her.

He was nearly as tall as Christina, and he had rumpled red hair. His thin arms poked out of a blue T-shirt. His hands were stuffed into the pockets of his blue jeans, which were frayed at the hem and worn through the knees. Scuffed tennis shoes completed his look.

"This is Erick," Christina said.

"Hi." Kylie couldn't think of anything else to say.

"Erick, as we've discussed at length, this is your biological mother, Kylie Killian."

The boy looked her over then turned his attention to his own shoes. "Hi."

"This is kind of weird, huh?" Kylie asked. "I'm not sure what to say or do."

"Why don't we just sit down and talk for a bit?" Christina suggested as she pulled out a chair at the table.

"Sure." Kylie sat down on the opposite side of the table.

"Whatever," Erick mumbled and sat at the end of the table,

as far from Kylie and Christina as he could get, causing a pain in Kylie's chest.

Christina glanced at the file folder in front of her on the table. "You're an artist?"

Kylie stole a look at Erick, who stared down at the table. "Yeah. I like to draw. I taught for a semester at Interlochen. It's a boarding school for high school artists in Michigan. I'm also a freelance designer."

Erick glowered at her then spoke. "Why are you here now? Why do you care about me now but not when I was born?"

The hostility in his voice shouldn't have surprised Kylie, but it still made her question the possibility of him ever wanting to have a relationship with her. "Fair enough. I didn't give you up for adoption. I was told by the nurses at Middleton—where you were born—that you'd died of pneumonia. I wanted you. I knew my life would be hard, but I loved you, and I wanted to keep you."

"Likely story."

"I understand if you're upset with me. I've been pretty upset myself since I found out you were alive." She shook her head and cleared her throat. "Not upset that you're alive, upset that I was lied to. Upset that someone else got to raise you."

"And what do you want now?"

To take you home and get to know you. She couldn't tell him that because she didn't want to overwhelm him. She wished Tom was next to her, holding her hand. Even though he wasn't Erick's biological father, the two of them had always been linked in her mind. "I don't know."

"You don't want me?"

"I don't know. I'm still in shock that you've been found. I…" She ran her hands through her hair. "What do you want?"

"I want my parents back. I want them to be alive." His lower lip trembled, and he blinked furiously before turning away to face the window.

Kylie swallowed her disappointment. Erick had no reason to want to have a relationship with her. "That would be ideal, wouldn't it?" When he didn't respond, she said, "I'd like to get to know you if that's okay."

"I suppose." He pushed back from the table. "I have to go. I have a lot of homework tonight."

Christina quickly stood and blocked him from leaving. "I'm sure your homework can wait a bit longer."

Kylie didn't want to force him to stay. Right now, she wasn't even sure she wanted to stay any longer. It was all she could do not to sob at the sadness in his voice and on his face. She wanted to hug him and comfort him but didn't feel as though she had the right since they barely knew each other. "No, that's fine. I totally understand how awkward and strange this must be for him. I'm at a loss myself." She stood and crossed the room to hand Erick one of her business cards. "If you decide you want to talk to me, just let me know. My email is on there and so is my cell number."

Erick took the card, glanced at it, and tucked it into his pocket. With a nod of his head, he walked away.

Kylie cleared her throat, hoping that she sounded nearly normal when she turned to Christina. "Is it possible that I can get a current photo of him? I only have one from when he was three days old."

Christina nodded and dabbed at her eyes with a crumpled tissue. "I thought you might ask for one, so I brought a copy of his last school photo."

Kylie sank into the chair Erick had vacated and gazed at his photo. "Am I doing the right thing?" she asked.

"I think so. I appreciate you taking time to get to know him before you tell him you want to be his mother."

Kylie frowned at Christina. "I don't know how to be a mother. I never had a chance to learn. I'm not sure I'm the best option for him, but I doubt anyone could love him more than I do."

"It's okay. Nothing is being decided right now. He'll stay with the foster family he's currently with. You're in a very uncommon position right now. It's normal to be confused. It's clear you want the best for him by putting his feelings and desires before your own."

Kylie nodded. "I do want what's best for him, but what if he never calls me? Will you keep me posted on him? Maybe we can schedule another meeting in a month or so?" She forced herself to smile. "Maybe if he sees I really am interested, he'll be more willing."

Christina patted her hand. "Of course, dear. We'd love to

see the two of you reunited, even if it takes a while to build up to that relationship."

Kylie was okay with waiting, but she was terrified that Erick would decide she wasn't worth the bother of getting to know. He seemed like a well-behaved child, and the misery in his face at any mention of his adoptive parents made it pretty clear he'd been raised with love.

Chapter 28

TOM SMILED AND hugged Emily. "Thanks for coming to stay with me for a while. It was a lot of fun."

She put her arms around his neck and squeezed tightly. "I don't want to go."

"You have to go with your mom, but you'll always be my friend."

"Can I come back and visit you?"

"We'll see." Tom would love to spend time with Emily. He was already worried that Eva would ditch the kid for her next fling. The only problem with maintaining a relationship with Emily was that Eva would think it meant they were still in a relationship.

"Maybe you can come stay with Tom some weekend," Eva said.

Tom nodded. "Sure. We can figure something out."

Eva smiled and slid her hand up Tom's arm. "Maybe we both can spend a weekend with Tom."

Tom pried Emily from his neck and handed her to Eva. "I don't think that's a good idea."

"Why not?" Emily asked.

"Your mom and I aren't very good friends anymore, and I'm upset with her. You're welcome to visit me anytime, Emily. Your mom isn't as welcome."

Eva frowned and set Emily down. "Fine. Get your bag, Emily. It's time to go."

"Don't blame her, Eva. You're the one who lied to me."

"I just don't get why you care so suddenly about being lied to. It's been going on for years, and it never bothered you."

"Yeah, well, you're not Kylie, and you purposely lied to me."

"What makes you think she didn't lie to you purposely?"

Tom opened the door and noted the shiny black SUV waiting. "Good point. Either way, you and I are through. Take care, Emily."

Emily nodded and grabbed him around the waist. Unable to deny himself a last hug, he hoisted her in his arms. As her tears soaked his collar, he whispered to her. "If you ever need anything, you call me, okay?"

Emily nodded.

"You remember my phone number, right?"

She nodded again. He squeezed his eyes shut and buried his nose in her hair, swallowing his own tears. "You're going to be fine."

He opened the back door of the SUV and buckled her into the car seat then backed away as Eva got into the front seat without another word to him.

Chapter 29

THREE DAYS AFTER meeting Erick, Kylie opened her door to find Lance standing on her porch in his uniform. "Hey, what's up?" she asked.

He wouldn't meet her gaze. "You need to come in to the station."

Kylie crossed her arms and held her elbows in her hands as she leaned against the door frame. "Why? What's going on?"

"We need you to answer some questions."

Confused, she couldn't think of anything she would need to talk to the police about. "Is it about Erick?"

"I can't answer that." Lance turned to the left, avoiding her gaze.

"Is this official?"

After sighing, he nodded.

She straightened up from the doorframe. "Are you arresting me?"

He shook his head. "Just escorting you in for questioning."

"I'll take myself to the station." If she drove herself, she could leave at any time.

Lance indicated the police car behind him, and Kylie saw another officer in the driver's seat. "I can't let you do that."

She narrowed her eyes at him. "This seems a little out of the realm of standard procedure. What's going on?"

"It's a small town. I heard about the order to bring you in and called in a couple of favors so I could do it. I thought it might be easier for you."

She didn't make any move to indicate she was going to cooperate. She wasn't even convinced that Lance wasn't playing some sort of joke on her. She hadn't done anything to warrant being hauled down to the police station. "About what?"

"I have no idea, Kylie. Please, can you just grab whatever you need and come with? I don't want to cuff you, but if I have to, I will." He wouldn't meet her gaze and seemed awfully interested in the door behind her.

Kylie swallowed. It must be serious if he would cuff her to bring her to the station. He clearly knew what was going on but didn't want to tell her. "Fine. Let me grab my keys."

Lance nodded once and stepped inside.

After sliding her feet into a pair of shoes, she pulled on a jacket and plucked her keys from the counter. "All right. Let's get this over with."

Lance waited on the step while she locked the door. He opened the rear door of the cruiser, and Kylie got in, more curious than concerned. The driver never looked at her, but he nodded when Lance got in beside him and fastened his seat belt.

"Should I have a lawyer?" she asked.

"I don't know," Lance replied. "Do you want one?"

She shook her head, convinced this was just a misunderstanding. "I guess I'll have to wait and see what this is all about before I can make a decision on that."

The squad car was silent on the way to the police station, other than the squawk and gibberish coming from the radio.

At the police station, Lance led her into a small conference room with a table and several chairs. The officer from the squad car followed them. Lance indicated a chair for Kylie, and she sat across from a man wearing a brown suit and a tie covered with tiny mallards.

"What's going on?" she asked.

"I'm Detective Smith. I'd like to know where you were on Tuesday evening."

Kylie thought back. Tuesday was the day after she'd met Erick. "I was home. In my attic. Drawing." She'd worked on a picture of Erick, relieved that he looked more like her than his father.

"Is there anyone to confirm that?"

Kylie shook her head. "No. Does there need to be?"

"How do you know Vernon Tallbaum?"

Kylie cocked her head and swallowed as her palms started to sweat. "We went to the same school, like everyone else in this town."

"How do you and Mr. Tallbaum get along?"

"We don't. I avoid him." It wasn't easy in a town the size of

Chinkapin, but she could count the number of times they'd interacted since she was fifteen.

"Why?"

"Because I don't like him." She shrugged. "That's not a crime, is it?"

"Why don't you like him?"

Kylie narrowed her eyes. "What's going on here?"

Lance cleared his throat and glanced at the detective. The detective nodded, and Lance said, "Vern was assaulted. He has a severe concussion and some facial fractures. He claims you did it."

Kylie narrowed her eyes. She would address Lance's lie later. "Not a chance that I did it. He's substantially larger than me, and I wouldn't get close enough to him to hurt him."

Detective Smith's frown deepened as he leaned forward and rested his forearms on the table. "Did you hire someone to do it?"

Kylie shook her head in disbelief. "What the hell for?"

"He claims you have plenty of reasons to want him dead."

Kylie rolled her eyes. "Just because I have reasons to want it doesn't mean I did it."

"What reasons?"

Realizing how serious the detective and Lance were, Kylie shook her head. "Nothing. I was joking. I had nothing to do with it."

She met the detective's gaze evenly. She couldn't look at Lance, afraid she might cry. He had known why they were bringing her in and lied to her about it. If he believed she was innocent, he wouldn't have lied and would be defending her now.

Finally, the detective pushed back from the table and stood. "I suggest you stick around town until this is cleared up, Miss Killian."

"Does that mean I'm under arrest? Or just a suspect?"

"It means I want you to be available if we have more questions."

Detective Smith exited the room, leaving her with Lance.

"I'll give you a ride home. My shift just finished." Lance led her out of the building to his Jeep, eyes straight ahead, jaw clenched.

"Convenient that they kept you around long enough to be a part of that."

Lance frowned. "It wasn't like that. I requested it."

"Why? Do you like watching people humiliate me?" Kylie could only remember one time she'd felt more humiliated.

"No, I thought it might be easier for you if I was there."

She yanked open the passenger door and got in, slamming the door as hard as she could. "Why? So I could see that you believe I did it?"

"Dammit, Kylie. I care about you. You should know that by now."

Staring out the window, she nearly spat the next words as he started the Jeep. "I also know you're a cop, and I was just questioned. I'm not sure where your loyalties lie."

"Why don't you tell me what happened so I can help you?"

"What makes you think something happened?"

"Vern's barely alive and thinks you arranged it. You even admitted you had plenty of reason to do it. You seem different lately. If you're not involved, why aren't you telling me the truth?"

Kylie scowled. "So what you're saying is it's me against him because his mother's a judge. You don't think the son of a judge would ever lie? Am I understanding correctly?"

"Vern said the only person he could think of that would want to hurt him is you."

"That's bullshit."

"Really?"

"There are other people who'd want to hurt him."

"Such as?"

Kylie shook her head. "Never mind." It wasn't her place to tell Lance that Vern had been in the group who'd raped Mira. When Mira had been raped, she hadn't told anyone. When Kylie had been raped by Vernon Tallbaum a few weeks later, she didn't say anything either. She didn't want her parents to know she'd snuck out that night to meet Tom, and she hadn't wanted Tom to know what had happened to her. Now, she wished she'd had a backbone and reported him.

"It's my job to find out."

"Really? You're an investigator? I thought you were just a lowly beat cop."

Lance narrowed his eyes as he glanced at her before turning into her driveway. "I suppose you should find a lawyer."

"Why?"

"Vern claims you have a good reason to want him dead."

"Are you out of your mind?" She couldn't believe Vern would actually tell people why Kylie would want him dead. He wasn't smart, but he couldn't be that stupid.

He shook his head and pulled up next to her porch. "Are *you*?"

Kylie glared at him. As she watched him, his expression softened.

He touched her hand. "Why would Vern say you had a good reason?"

"Because I do," she admitted quietly. "But I didn't have anything to do with him being beaten."

Lance grabbed her hand and met her gaze. "Tell me what's going on. Not as a cop, but as your friend."

"And how's that going to be used? Aren't you obligated or sworn to uphold the law?"

"Of course I am, but you didn't break the law. Did you?"

Kylie cast her eyes down to her lap and shook her head. If she really wanted to remain friends with Lance, she had to tell him everything. She took a deep breath and twisted her hands together. "He raped me."

Lance clenched his fist. "What? I'll kill him."

Kylie shook her head. "It wasn't recently."

He turned the key to start the Jeep. "Let's go."

She grabbed his arm to stop him. "Where do you think we're going?"

"You're going to report this. I'll arrest his sorry ass, and the charges against you will be dropped."

"Really? Don't be ridiculous. It was years ago, and all it'll do is convince everyone I did have a reason to do what he claims I did."

"How long ago?"

Kylie met his gaze and blinked, surprised he hadn't made the connection. "It was when I was fifteen."

"When you were dating Tom?"

Kylie nodded and bit the inside of her cheek.

His eyes widened as he drew back. "And he's Erick's father?

That's why you didn't tell Tom the truth?"

"I didn't want to believe he was Erick's father. I convinced myself that I couldn't have gotten pregnant by him. It was just the one time, and Tom and I had sex multiple times." She grabbed his hand. "But I didn't do anything to him. I didn't hire anyone to beat him. I haven't done anything in eleven years. I don't know who got pissed at Vernon. I'm sure he deserved everything that happened to him, but I had nothing to do with it." She ran her hands through her hair. "I really don't understand why he mentioned me. He has to know if it goes to trial that the truth about what happened is going to come out."

"He's not very bright. Never has been. Maybe he thinks you'll leave town instead of telling the truth."

Kylie threw her hands up in the air. "It doesn't matter. Even if I tell what happened, like I said, everyone's just going to say it proves I had a motive. Don't forget his mother is a judge."

"Crap. You really do need a lawyer. A good one."

"Why? Whatever happens happens. I'm glad he got the crap beat out of him. If I really thought I could get away with it, I would have done it. If I get charged with assault, so what? I disappear from Chinkapin, and everyone's problems are tied up with a neat little bow."

"Everyone's problems?"

"Vern won't have to worry about me telling anyone. His family stays intact. The Mallocks won't have to worry about me sullying their name, and my family can continue pretending I don't exist." She shrugged, refusing to let the tears fall. "Seems like winning all around."

Lance reached out and pulled her into his arms. "Except for you."

"Who says I wouldn't be winning? Maybe I could cut ties with this town for good then instead of mistakenly coming back and thinking everything will be better this time."

He caressed her hair. "We can beat this."

His arms felt so good. "I don't want you to be involved. It can't be good for your career to be hanging out with me, anyway."

"Fuck my career. I'm a cop. That doesn't mean I can't be your friend."

"Well, I don't know what the answer is. I guess I'll just wait for the public defender to contact me."

"That's not a good move."

"How do you know? Have you used them before?" Kylie found it easier to argue with him about every little thing than to admit she was scared. She didn't want to go to prison for something she didn't do, but she didn't want to let everyone know how messed up she was over this.

When she shivered, Lance turned off the Jeep and ushered her inside. She sat on the sofa and wrapped a blanket around her shoulders, while he stacked kindling in the fireplace.

"Are you okay? Seriously?"

"No, not even a little okay. I really just want to leave town and never come back. Mexico sounds nice."

Lance met her gaze and smiled sadly. "You can beat this. Let me help."

"I don't know how you're going to help me. I have no alibi, yet I have plenty of motive. I'm screwed."

"What if we figure out who did it?"

"I don't want to put you in a difficult position with your job."

"I'm pretty sure I know someone who can help. Will you let me ask them on your behalf?"

Kylie screwed her mouth to the side and after a moment, she nodded. It's not as if she had anything to lose.

* * *

The next day, Kylie looked up from washing dishes and saw Tom walking up her steps. "What do you want?" she asked when she opened the door. She crossed her arms and leaned against the door frame, making it obvious she wasn't about to invite him inside.

"Lance called me."

"So?"

He didn't smile, but he wasn't frowning either. "He told me you need a lawyer."

Kylie was still struggling to figure out how to convince the detective she was innocent. "He seems to think so."

"What do you think?"

Kylie frowned. "He's probably right. I don't know why he

called you, though."

"My college roommate is a defense lawyer. I called him this morning, and he'll be calling you later today or tomorrow. He'll take your case."

"How does he know he'll take my case? He doesn't know anything about it."

"I told him what I knew."

She couldn't stop herself from asking, "And that was what?"

Tom glared at the floor. "That asshole raped you when you were fifteen. Someone beat the crap out of him, and for some reason, he's blaming you."

Kylie turned away, hoping to hide the tears that ran down her face.

He reached out and touched her shoulder then let his hand drop. "Look, Kylie. I'm sorry that I was a jackass about Erick. I should have known that you wouldn't have cheated on me. I guess I was just in shock."

She turned back and was dumbfounded to see the tears on his face. "I was flabbergasted too."

"Why didn't you tell me? Ever?"

"I didn't want to be pregnant at all, and since I was, I definitely didn't want him to be the father. I convinced myself that you were the father. I had no idea until the DNA test came back." She took a deep breath and backed up. "Come on in. We might as well sit down while you question me."

"I'm not questioning you. I just don't understand why I didn't know. I would have—"

"What would you have done, Tom?"

"I would have made sure he paid for it."

"It doesn't really matter. Erick's not your son, so you don't have to worry about being a dad anymore." She looked out the window, not sure she could handle seeing his response. If he looked relieved, she would be angry. If he looked upset, she would cry because that was all she wanted to do right now.

"You have to believe that I'm sorry for the way I acted at the investigator's office."

She nodded. "Sure."

"No, don't just say 'sure.' Either accept my apology or don't, but at least acknowledge that I regret how I acted."

"I know, Tom. It was a shock to both of us. I forgive you."

After a few minutes of uncomfortable silence, Tom asked, "So have you met Erick?"

"Yeah. He wasn't interested in getting to know me." She pulled Erick's latest school picture from the pocket of her jeans. She'd kept it on her body since she'd received it, taking it out at random times. "I have a picture of him if you want to see."

He held his hand out, and she placed the picture in it, hoping he wouldn't say that Erick looked like his father.

"He looks like you. Same hair and eyes."

Kylie smiled. "Poor kid to end up with my hair."

"Your hair is beautiful. It always has been." Tom handed the picture back. "I believe you, Kylie. I don't think you had anything to do with Vern's assault. Although, if I'd known what he'd done, he wouldn't be alive to be assaulted." He clenched his fists and raised them as he spun around and paced to the other side of the kitchen. For a moment, Kylie thought he might punch the wall, but instead, he took a deep breath and blew it out before he turned back.

Kylie forced herself to smile. "That's probably part of why I never told you. I didn't want you to get into trouble."

"Don't be ridiculous. I'm a Mallock. I would have hired the best lawyer I could find." He took a deep breath. "Look, I know you're not going to be happy about this, but you were mentioned in the paper today. Just listed in the article about the assault as 'a female suspect' who has been questioned."

"I'm a suspect now? Don't they have to arrest me and charge me before they refer to me as a suspect?" Kylie wished she knew more about the legal process. She even wished Lance was there so she could ask him what the hell was going on.

"I don't know. Be sure to ask your lawyer when he calls you. Maybe you can sue the police department and newspaper for defamation of character."

"Not likely since they didn't list my name." She shrugged. "Whatever. Things are going to get a whole lot uglier around here for me when the truth comes out."

"Just remember, you have friends. We've got your back."

Kylie sniffled and wiped at her tears. "Thanks, Tom. It means a lot."

He stepped closer and reached for her again. This time she stood still as he wrapped his arms around her. "I'm so sorry," he whispered into her hair. "I never should have doubted you. Not when you disappeared, not when you returned, not when I found out Erick wasn't my kid."

"What about when I told you Eva was lying?"

"Definitely shouldn't have doubted you about that." He cleared his throat. "She admitted it to me, then she and Emily left."

Kylie slowly brought her hands up to his waist, and as her quiet tears turned to sobs, she buried her face against the chest of his red sweatshirt. "I'm sorry too," she whispered.

His hand traveled up and down her spine. "Did you ever tell anyone what happened?"

She shook her head against his chest. "What good would it have done? His mother is a judge."

"And you think that he'd have gotten off?"

"I didn't want to talk about what had happened."

"So that week when you didn't want to be around me…"

She nodded. "I didn't want to be around anyone, but then, when I did agree to see you, it was wonderful, and you made me forget about what he'd done." She gripped his sweatshirt tightly in her fists, trying to control her tears. "I'm sorry."

He stepped back and brought his hands up to cup her face then tipped it up to meet his gaze. "You don't have anything to be sorry about."

She blinked until her vision cleared and stared into his blue eyes. "I never stopped loving you, Tom. Not even when you hated me," she whispered.

"I never hated you." He bowed his head and brushed his lips over hers then pulled away to check her response.

She grinned. "Yeah, you did, and I understand why."

He cocked his head and grinned back. "Maybe a little bit."

She slid her hands to his chest and rose up on her tiptoes to press her lips to his. This time, it wasn't a gentle kiss; it was more like the hot kisses they'd shared on New Year's Eve. When they broke apart, she asked, "You're sure that you and Eva are through?"

"Definitely," he replied and pulled her to the living room, where they sank into the recliner together.

Chapter 30

THE NEXT EVENING, Tom let himself into Kylie's house. "I brought supper," he called.

"What did you get?" Kylie asked as she entered the kitchen. She'd been in the attic, drawing a picture of herself with Tom and Erick.

"Burgers, fries, and beer. Sound good?"

"Burgers sound great."

As he carried the paper bag to the table, Kylie got plates and glasses from the cabinet. When she turned, he was opening the bottles of beer, and she focused on his hands. She'd always loved his hands. Before she'd met Tom, she never noticed hands on a guy, but his hands were gentle and capable. The more time she spent watching his hands, the sexier they became to her.

Kylie sat down. "What's up?"

His gaze shifted to the window and back to her. "Just curious how things are with Erick."

"They aren't. I left my info with him in case he wanted to get in touch, but I'm not going to force anything."

Tom rubbed the back of his neck.

Kylie pursed her lips. "You think I should spend more time with him."

He took a big swallow of his beer before nodding. "I do."

Her stomach twisted, and her appetite disappeared. Without speaking, she hugged herself. "Why?"

"Don't you want to have a relationship with him?"

"Yes." Kylie picked up her bottle of beer and finished it. Slamming the bottle down on the counter, she gazed at Tom while tears burned her eyes. "Of course I do. I want to know everything about him. I want to hug him every night before bed, every morning when he wakes up, and multiple times throughout the day simply because I can, but I refuse to force him into something. I want to do what he wants."

"Maybe you're too worried about Erick and not considering your own feelings."

"My own feelings don't matter. We can't all act on our feelings. Someone has to be a responsible adult. He's old enough to know what he wants. I'm not going to argue with that."

"I'm not trying to argue with that. I just want to know what you really want without four hundred conditions. It's okay to want what you want. You don't need Erick's permission to want to be a part of his life."

"I don't want to argue about it anymore. I will do whatever Erick wants in this situation."

"I get it. I understand. I just wanted to know."

"Why does it matter so much?"

"I love you, Kylie. I want to marry you, and I want you to know that if you'll let me, I want to adopt Erick. I don't care who his father is. I only care that he's yours, and that you love him."

Kylie froze. She'd been fantasizing about a happily ever after with Tom and Erick ever since the first time he'd kissed her. She'd barely been able to stop herself from sketching a wedding dress. "What? You want to marry me?"

"Why are you so surprised? Of course I want to marry you. As soon as possible. I didn't mean to spring it on you like this. I had a plan that was supposed to be romantic."

"Wow." Kylie's knees buckled, and she sank into a chair as she brought her hands up to her mouth. She could hardly believe her ears. There was so much going on that would make her less than appealing as a wife, yet Tom had just proposed.

He lowered himself to the floor in front of her, pulled a small box from his pocket, and opened it. "Kylie Killian, will you marry me?"

"Wow," she repeated as he lifted her hand and slid the gold band with a single diamond onto her finger.

"Please?"

"Yes," she whispered. They'd talked about this when they were in high school. Over the years, the memory of their discussions had faded, but here it was—the simple ring she'd told him she wanted when she was fifteen.

"When?"

"Any time you want." She admired the ring for a second then raised her gaze to his smiling face. He had a few more wrinkles around his eyes but otherwise looked the same as when they'd first met. "I had no idea you would do this."

"I spent the past eleven years wishing I knew where you and our baby were. Now that I've found you and you've forgiven me for being a stupid ass, I'm not going to let you just walk away. I know it's early, and I'm pretty sure we'll have hard times, but we can get through anything."

"Are you sure you don't just want to date for a while and see what happens? We could live together."

"Nope, I want the whole enchilada."

"And marriage is the whole enchilada?"

He shook his head. "No, not quite."

"So what is the whole enchilada?"

"The whole enchilada is having both of our families over for holidays and having them all spoil our kids."

Kylie gasped as her stomach sank. "Kids?"

"Don't you want kids?" he asked gently.

"I don't know." She shook her head. "I haven't really thought about it since we found Erick. When I thought he was dead, I didn't want any other kids. I only wanted him, and since we found out he was alive, I've been trying to figure out what I wanted to do about him. Now, I've met him, and I'm just waiting and hoping he'll decide he wants me to be part of his life." She leaned forward to kiss him. "I love you. I want to be your wife. I just don't know how I feel about kids other than Erick right now."

"I understand, and it's perfectly fine. I want to spend the rest of my life with you, and I'd like for us to consider the possibility of children."

"I'll consider it. That's all I can offer you at this point."

He cradled her face in his hands then leaned forward to kiss her gently. "That's all I'm asking for."

"Why are you so good to me?"

"Because you deserve it, and I love you."

With a smile, she took his hand and led him upstairs to the studio where she'd wanted to give him her virginity. She was determined to do everything in her power to make tonight a night they would never forget.

Chapter 31

LATER THAT EVENING, Tom and Kylie sat on the sofa in the attic studio. Neither of them was speaking; they were just hanging out together. Tom's arm was around Kylie's shoulders, and her head rested on his shoulder.

"I need to find out who beat Vern," she whispered.

"Why?"

"Because there's no way I can prove I didn't do it. I need to convince whoever did it to admit to it."

"Why would someone admit to a crime if they're already getting away with it?"

Kylie patted his chest. "I don't know, but I can't just sit here and hope that if it goes to trial, your friend is as good as you think he is." She looked around and sighed. "Oh, and I should get this place cleaned up to sell."

"Why are you selling it?"

She laughed. "I need to pay the lawyer somehow."

"No, it's pro bono. He agreed to do it as a favor to me." He wasn't about to tell her that he'd already sent his friend a substantial check to cover expenses.

"That's nice of him." Her voice was distracted.

He doubted she'd even heard him because the Kylie he knew wouldn't accept charity so easily.

"Do you know anyone who'd be mad enough at Vern to beat him?" Kylie asked.

"Tallbaum? I'm sure there's tons of people." He stared at the wall in front of him. "You know, he was bugging some bartender on New Year's Eve. Right before you came out of the bathroom." He leaned to the side and gazed at her. "He's why you were so jumpy that night when you came out of the bathroom, right?"

"I didn't know he was harassing anyone. Who was it?"

"I just meant you were nervous because you knew he was there, and you were alone in a relatively uninhabited part of the bar."

She nodded. "Who was it?"

"I don't know her name. She had dark hair and was in the stock room. I went looking for you and heard her yelling at him to leave her alone. She swore there wasn't anything wrong, though."

Kylie leapt to her feet and grabbed her jeans from the floor. "I need to go," she said as she shimmied them up her legs.

He pulled her to stand between his legs. "I'd rather you stayed here with me."

"Later. I need to talk to that woman."

"What makes you think she's at the bar?"

"You said she works there. Someone will know her name and where to find her."

"You sure?"

"Why wouldn't they?"

"They'll know, but they might not tell you. Do you really think Scott will confide in you?"

She gathered her hair in a knot at the back of her neck, and he frowned. He loved her hair when it was a riot around her face. When it was pulled back, it was hard to remember how wild she could be, just like her hair.

"Okay." He pulled his T-shirt and jeans back on before standing. "Let's go."

"You don't have to come with."

"Of course I don't. I want to. Is that okay?" He wanted to leave her home and take care of this whole Tallbaum issue himself, but then he would probably end up in jail. Besides, he knew she wouldn't just sit back and watch.

She nodded at him and led him to the kitchen, where she grabbed her coat and shoved her feet into her boots.

"Is there any chance I can convince you to stay here and let me talk to Scott?" he asked, already knowing the answer.

She smiled. "Is there any chance I can leave you here and take care of my own problems?"

He shook his head at her grin, and they walked out to his truck together.

On the way to the bar, he reached out and touched her hand, expecting her to pull away from him like she used to when she was concentrating on something. Instead, she brought his hand up to her mouth and kissed it. "Thank you."

"You're welcome, but I don't know what you're thanking me for."

"Understanding," she whispered.

"Thank you for forgiving me," he replied, still shocked that he was sitting next to her and holding her hand again. "I really missed you."

She smiled at him. "I know the feeling."

When they arrived at the bar, she released his hand and took a deep breath.

"Ready?" he asked.

She nodded. "Don't attack Scott if he doesn't want to cooperate."

"Me? What about you?"

"Yeah, don't attack me either."

Once inside, they crossed the nearly empty room to sit side by side at the bar.

"Her?" Kylie asked Tom as she gestured toward the purple-haired woman. When he nodded, she said, "I think she's dating Scott."

When the woman turned and saw Tom, she crossed over to him. "What can I get you?"

"I'll have a beer." He looked at Kylie. "Make that two beers."

"Sure thing." She turned to draw the beers, and Kylie started peering around the room. When she visibly relaxed, Tom realized how much she hated being out someplace where she might run into Tallbaum.

"Here you go. On the house." The waitress set the two mugs down in front of them. "You're Scott's sister, right?"

Kylie nodded. "We're, um…"

"Families are shit sometimes. I don't think he really hates you, but he won't tell me what happened between the two of you."

"You're Sunny, right?" Kylie asked.

The bartender nodded.

"Are you guys close?"

"Yeah. We've been dating for a few years."

Tom cocked his head. "Where is he?"

"In the stockroom. Why?"

"Just wondering." Tom touched Kylie's arm and waited until she looked at him. "You okay?"

She nodded then took a swallow of her beer. When she set her mug back down, she met the bartender's gaze. "Have you seen Vernon Tallbaum around here tonight?"

"No. He won't be back in here."

"Why not?" Tom asked.

"Scott beat the crap out of him the other night."

Kylie gasped. "Why?"

"Scott caught that asshole grabbing my ass in the hallway." Sunny frowned. "I should have just handled it myself."

Kylie reached across the bar and touched her hand. "I've been questioned about the attack. They're trying to charge me with assault."

"Yeah, that's the rumor we heard."

"Did you hear why I supposedly did it?" Kylie asked.

"Vern said that you kept asking him out and when he turned you down, you lost your mind."

Kylie cursed.

Tom closed his eyes and turned away, wishing for an instant that Tallbaum would walk into the bar so he could beat the shit out of him.

Kylie stood. "I need to talk to Scott."

Sunny reached across the bar and grabbed Kylie's arm. "You can't turn him in. He'll go to jail because of his past record."

"Kylie's looking at jail herself," Tom said. "And she's suffered enough at the hands of that asshole."

Sunny narrowed her eyes at Kylie. "How?"

"Never mind." Kylie turned to Tom and shook her head. "I'm just going to talk to my brother." She walked away without looking back.

When Tom turned back to Sunny, she asked, "What did he do to her?"

"It's not my place. She'll kill me if she finds out I told you."

"Not likely. If she wanted to kill you, she already would have."

Tom propped his forearms on the bar and leaned forward, wishing he could just turn back time twelve years. "I can't tell you, especially not here. Visit Kylie sometime and ask her."

Chapter 32

KYLIE MADE HER way down the hall and pushed on the door labeled "Employees Only." The door opened easily, and she saw her younger brother's back as he sorted through boxes.

She took a deep breath and let it out, trying to compose herself. "Hey, Scott." She pushed the door shut behind her as she stepped into the room.

He glanced over his shoulder. "I can't talk to you. I'm working."

"We need to talk."

"Not now."

"Dammit, Scott. You're not going to keep avoiding me. I want you to know what happened to me. I want you to know my side of the story. I don't know what you think happened when I left, but you need to know the truth." She took a deep breath again and forced her fists to relax.

"Since you obviously aren't going to walk out of here without talking to me, make it fast. My boss is coming in for inventory in a little bit."

"When I was fifteen, I was in a relationship with Tom Mallock. I lied to Mom and Dad about who I was with, because, as you know, they hated the Mallocks. One afternoon, I was hanging out with Tom, and he dropped me off a couple blocks from home. As I was walking home, Vern Tallbaum grabbed me and pulled me into an alley."

She stared at the floor, trying to work up her nerve to say the rest of it.

Scott turned away from the shelf of boxes and faced her. His shoes appeared in her line of vision. "What did he do to you?"

Tears seeped out of her eyes at the concern in his voice, concern she never thought Scott would have for her again. She held up one finger in a "just wait" gesture as she tried to control her emotions.

"Did he rape you?"

Kylie nodded and sighed heavily, so thankful she didn't have to say it herself. She wrapped her arms around her waist and hugged herself then forced her gaze to meet his, noting his black eye. "I got pregnant. I always thought it was Tom's baby. I convinced myself it was Tom's baby. We'd been having sex. Surely if I was pregnant, it would be Tom's. When I told Mom, she and Dad decided to send me to Middleton Girl's Home. I didn't even get to tell Tom good-bye."

She shuffled her feet. "When the baby, Erick, was born, I refused to give him up for adoption, but three days later, the nurses took him from me. I was sick, and they didn't want him to catch whatever I had, or so they said."

She swiped at the tears streaming down her face. "The next morning, I was told that Erick had died from pneumonia. For eleven years, I believed my son was dead. Mom and Dad shipped me off to Interlochen. I don't know if they honestly thought that would help me, or if they just didn't want me back in Chinkapin.

"Last summer, I found out our parents and Tom's parents had worked together to convince the people at Middleton to lie about Erick's death. He's alive somewhere."

She forced a humorless laugh out. "He's alive and without parents. Tom hired an investigator to find him. When they did a DNA test, it turned out that Erick wasn't Tom's baby. His father is Vernon Tallbaum."

"Holy shit," Scott whispered.

"He told the cops that I hired someone to beat him up. I've been questioned. He claims I'm the only one with a motive."

"And he wants everyone to know what that motive is?"

Kylie shuddered. "I don't know why he named me. He hates me, obviously."

"I can't confess, Kylie. I'll end up in jail."

Kylie stared at her brother's blue eyes, remembering how she used to cover for him whenever he got into trouble with their parents. Biting back a sob, she nodded. "I know. I just want you to know the truth. I want you to realize I didn't choose to leave you and Kristy. I didn't know about Kristy dying until well after the funeral. You have to forgive me."

Scott reached out and patted her shoulder awkwardly.

"Yeah."

Kylie sighed in relief. She had hoped for a hug from him, but she would take a pat and forgiveness.

He looked at his watch. "I have to get back out to the bar. Thanks for telling me the truth."

"Do you really forgive me? Or are you just saying it so I'll leave you alone?"

"I mean it. We'll get together one of these days and get caught up. Sunny wants to get to know you."

Kylie smiled. "Yeah, that sounds fun. Let me know when." She followed him out of the storage room and went directly into the bathroom down the hall. After locking herself in a stall, she sobbed.

She had wanted to find out who'd assaulted Vernon, but she didn't want her brother to go to jail for it. All she wanted was to have her family back and have her brother forgive her for all the things he thought she'd done.

Now, she knew she would never tell the truth about who beat Vern. She would keep her mouth shut and hope like hell that her lawyer could get her off, even if it meant she would go to jail.

Chapter 33

TOM AND KYLIE were sitting in her living room. They'd been watching TV together, but he noticed she was staring at the fireplace instead of the television.

He reached over and touched her hand.

She flinched then forced a smile. "Sorry. I was zoned out."

"No problem. Maybe you'll be able to get some sleep tonight."

"I'm fine. I've been sleeping."

Tom shook his head. "No, you haven't. Just like you haven't been eating. I doubt you've even been drawing."

She dropped her gaze to their connected hands. "I've been… You're right. I haven't been doing much of anything other than worrying."

"Why won't you tell me what you found out when you talked to Scott?"

"Nothing. I told him what really happened to me before I left town."

"You told him about Erick's fath—"

Her hand shot up to stop him. "He's not Erick's father."

"Technically, he is."

"He will never know Erick is his child. I don't care what else happens; I'm never going to tell him. He's never going to have a chance to talk to my son."

"What if Erick asks about his father?"

She shook her head angrily. "He's not going to know who his father is. I'll tell him I was raped. I won't tell him who did it."

Tom nodded. He didn't want to argue with her.

"What did Scott say when you told him?"

"That he's sorry and we should get together some time to catch up. Sunny wants to get to know me."

"What did he say about Tallbaum claiming you're the one who beat him?"

She shook her head. "I told you already. I'm not sending him to jail. If Scott is convicted of assault, he'll lose his job and end up in jail."

"You're willing to go to jail so he doesn't?"

She shifted away from him on the couch and crossed her arms. "You'd do the same for Lance."

"Don't bet on it." Tom wanted to think he would be selfless enough to take the blame for Lance if something like this happened, but he wasn't sure. He was sitting there with Lance's ex-girlfriend. It wasn't very believable, even to himself, that he would put his brother's best interests first. "I should just go finish the job."

"What job?" she asked.

"Beat Tallbaum to death."

"Don't be ridiculous. You're not going to do anything. We're finally together again, and I don't want you to end up in prison for murder."

He sighed. "Don't you get it? That's how I feel too."

Kylie shook her head. "Just let it be. Everything will be fine."

Just as Tom opened his mouth to argue more, her phone rang.

She picked up her cell phone and turned it so Tom could read "Lance" on the screen.

He shrugged.

"Hey, Lance. What's up?" She held Tom's gaze. "No. Tom's here."

Tom stood to leave. He didn't need or want to listen to her phone conversations.

Kylie reached out and grabbed his hand. "Just a second."

Tom didn't know if she was talking to him or to Lance until she tapped the screen of her phone.

"There, Lance. It's on speakerphone now. What's up?"

"I just wanted to tell you guys that there was a confession this afternoon. The police won't be questioning Kylie anymore about Tallbaum's assault."

"Who?" Kylie demanded.

"I can't tell you that. I shouldn't even be calling you. I just figured you deserved some good news for once."

"Was it Scott?" she asked.

Lance sighed through the phone. "I can't answer that, Kylie. I'm sorry. Your lawyer should be contacting you in the morning when the charges have been officially dropped."

Kylie slumped into the couch. "Dammit."

Tom reached out and took the phone from her hand. "Thanks for calling, Lance. I'll talk to you later."

"Sure thing." Lance's voice was strained. "Have a good night."

Tom ended the call. He knew exactly how Lance felt. It was the same way Tom had felt when he had woken from his coma and Kylie had moved away from him to kiss Lance.

"You okay?" Tom asked.

"I hope it wasn't Scott."

"Who else would it have been?"

"I don't know." Kylie shifted to rest her head on his chest. "I don't know that Scott and I will ever fix things. I'm done trying to force things with people who aren't interested."

He kissed the top of her head. "I'm interested, and you'll never have to force me."

"I'm not talking about you. Or us."

"Your family?"

"I'm done wasting my time with them."

"That's your choice." He waited a few minutes. "What about Erick?"

"I haven't heard from him since our first meeting."

"Are you going to see him again?"

"Yeah, probably in a few weeks. I don't want to push him."

Chapter 34

KYLIE GAZED OUT the window of her attic studio as snowflakes floated down. She'd been sitting upstairs for a couple of hours, but her sketch pad was unopened, and her pencils were resting next to her on the table as she tried to decide whether or not to sell her grandfather's house.

When her phone rang, she answered it without checking the caller ID. "Hello, this is Kylie." She hoped it might be one of her design clients with a project. She needed a distraction to take her mind off of Erick, Tom, and the house.

"Um, is this Kylie Killian?" The voice was young.

"Yes. Who is this?" Her heart raced, and she tried to control her excitement, telling herself not to jump to conclusions. There was no reason to believe Erick would actually call her.

"Erick Seversen. Um, I mean, Erick."

Unable to speak, Kylie nodded. It took her a moment to recover from the shock. "Hi there. How are you?"

"I'm okay. Why didn't my father come with you to see me?"

She swallowed. The moment she'd been dreading had finally arrived. "Your biological father and I weren't dating. We're not…" She grimaced. She didn't want to tell an eleven-year-old that he'd been conceived during a rape. "We're not close."

"Why?"

"Could we maybe get together and talk about this? It's not something I want to get into on the phone."

After a few seconds and a dramatic sigh, he said, "I suppose. When do you want to do it?"

"Are you busy tomorrow after school?"

* * *

An hour later, Kylie took a deep breath as Tom came into her kitchen and sat down at the table. "Erick called me earlier today. He wants to know who his father is."

"And?"

"I told him that I wasn't in a relationship with his father." She ran a hand over her face. "I couldn't tell him that I was raped, but he wants more info."

"Isn't that normal?"

"I have no idea. I'm not adopted. Even though my parents are mostly worthless, at least I know exactly who they are. What kid wants to know that his father is a rapist?" Kylie pulled away, the same way she did any time Vern came up in conversation.

"I think you should tell him the truth."

"Don't you think it's bad enough that he thinks I didn't love him enough to make sacrifices to keep him? Now you want me to tell him I didn't even want to have sex when he was conceived?"

"I think you should tell him the truth. I think he's old enough to know, especially since he asked."

She twisted her fingers around his then nodded. "You're probably right, but I've spent the last eleven years avoiding telling anyone I'd been raped. Now I have to tell my son, who doesn't even like me, the truth." They sat together for a few more minutes. "Will you come with me?"

"To talk to Erick?"

"You don't have to. I understand if you're not willing to."

"Don't be ridiculous. Of course I'll come with you. I'm just surprised that you're asking me for help. You seldom let anyone, even me, in when you're tackling difficult decisions."

"I figured it was time to try something new."

"I'm glad you're trying it with me, but what if he doesn't like me?"

Kylie chuckled at his nervousness. "Welcome to my world, Tom. All I've been doing is worrying about whether or not he'll like me."

* * *

Kylie and Tom entered the conference room at the social services building and sat side by side. She squeezed his hand tightly when the door opened, hoping he would remain calm and not let on how upset he'd been when he found out he wasn't Erick's father.

"Is this him?" Erick asked as he walked into the room.

Kylie shook her head. "No, this is Tom, my…"

"We're engaged," Tom said. "I'm glad to finally meet you, Erick."

"I'm sure."

"What's that mean?" Tom asked.

"I'm sure you're thrilled to meet the kid your fiancé gave up for adoption. It has to be high on your list of things to do."

"Actually, it was. I don't really care who your father is. You're part of Kylie, and that makes me eager to get to know you."

Erick narrowed his eyes. "I don't believe you."

Kylie placed her hand on Tom's arm as her heart swelled then constricted again. "Tom, don't."

"Don't what?" Erick asked.

"I don't want him to pressure you to get to know us. Or me. It's your decision. I already told you that."

"You'll respect my decision about that but not about meeting my dad?"

She took a deep breath and nodded. "It's not that I don't respect your decision. It's more that I've spent eleven years denying you're his child, for my own comfort and sanity, and it's not something I want to talk about."

Erick watched her with a distrustful expression.

Before she lost her nerve, she gripped Tom's hand again. "I was raped, Erick. When I was fifteen, I was dating Tom, and I was in love with him." She glanced at Tom, but all he did was squeeze her hand.

"One night, I was walking home from a date with him, and a guy I knew from school grabbed me, dragged me into an alley, and forced me to have sex with him. When I found out I was pregnant, I convinced myself that the baby—you—were Tom's. When Tom's investigator found you and ordered a DNA test, we found out that Tom isn't your father."

Erick's eyes bugged out. "But you know who my father is?"

Kylie swallowed repeatedly before she nodded. "I do."

"Do you know where he is?"

Kylie nodded again. "He lives in the same town I grew up in."

"Are you going to tell me who he is?"

She'd hoped telling him his father was a rapist would be enough. She didn't want to say Vern's name. She glanced at Tom, who squeezed her hand and nodded.

She took a deep breath. "His name is Vernon Tallbaum. He lives in Chinkapin."

"I want to meet him."

"Why?" Kylie whispered. "You don't want anything to do with me, yet you want to meet him? Why?"

"Because he's my father."

Kylie wiped the tears from her eyes, trying to ignore the fact that her son had just rejected her but wanted to meet the man who'd fathered him. "I talked to your social worker about it, and she thinks I should tell him, but I can't make any promises that he's going to be anything like you're hoping."

"He doesn't know about me?"

"No. I didn't think he deserved to know, but if you want to meet him, I'll see what I can do."

"I'll talk to him," Tom offered.

"Are you friends with him?" Erick asked.

"Definitely not," Tom replied.

Kylie shook her head. "I'll do it." She swiped at her face again, trying to control the tears. Speaking to Vernon was the last thing she wanted to do, but she wasn't about to make Tom do it. "Give me a minute, and I'll call him."

"You know his number?" Erick's eyes narrowed. "But you just said you're not friends."

"I have it in case that was what you wanted today." She rose from her chair, keeping her hand on the table to steady herself. "I'm going to go out in the hall for a few minutes. I'll be right back after I talk to him."

"No. Do it here."

Kylie froze, only her eyes shifting to look at Erick. "Why?"

Tom shook his head. "Come on, Erick. That's not fair. Kylie's done nothing to make you doubt her honesty. Let her have a little privacy."

Kylie stared into eyes that mirrored her own and knew she would do just about anything to have a relationship with Erick, even if it meant humiliating herself in front of him. When he didn't answer Tom, she said, "Fine. Let's do it right now." She scrolled through her phone to the contact she'd added earlier that morning, tapped the screen to call, and switched to speakerphone.

"Hello. Tallbaum and Associates. How may I help you?" The voice was smooth and polite, yet it grated on Kylie's nerves.

"This is Kylie Killian. I want to talk to Vernon Tallbaum."

"He's out of the office right now. Can I take a message?"

Kylie focused on Tom, who stared back at her with a gentle smile of encouragement on his face. "If he doesn't want me to sue him for defamation of character, you better figure out how to forward this call and ensure that he accepts it."

"One moment, please."

After a two-minute wait, the hold music stopped. "Tallbaum."

"This is Kylie Killian, but I'm sure your secretary told you that." She sank back into the chair she'd vacated. Her knees were shaking too hard for her to remain standing.

"What do you want? More of me?"

Tom growled, and Kylie's blood ran cold.

"Hardly. There's someone here who wants to meet you."

"Who? Your friend? What's her name again? Didn't she just marry your cousin? I wonder if he measures up to me."

"Good lord, you're an asshole." Kylie glanced at Tom, who showed zero surprise to learn that Mira had been raped by the same louse.

"And you're calling me for what reason?"

"You remember that night in the alley?"

"Which night?"

Kylie swallowed repeatedly, trying to get the bile back down her throat before she vomited. "You raped me." She stared at Erick, ready to end the conversation at the first sign of him being overwhelmed.

He stared down at his hands, which were pressed against the table.

"To-may-toe, to-mah-toe."

Tom squeezed her hand as she continued. "I got pregnant. Your son wants to meet you."

"Bullshit."

"Bullshit, what?"

"I'm not meeting any bastard child that you're trying to claim as mine. Everyone knows that you're working your way through the Mallocks. Surely, you can convince one of them that he's the father."

Tom pushed back from the table and reached for the phone. "Listen, Tallbaum, you piece of—"

Kylie swallowed hard and raised her hand toward Tom, trying to calm him. "Lord knows my son's life would be better off not sharing any DNA with you, but that's not the case. He wants to meet you."

Erick's face paled, and he clenched his fists.

"Not happening. I don't have any interest in any kid you've put up to demanding child support for."

"Come on. Don't be a dick. He wants to meet you. I promise I didn't want to make this call."

Erick cleared his throat and swiped at the tears under his eyes. "No, I don't. He sounds like a waste of oxygen."

Kylie's eyes widened before she smiled at Erick. "Fair enough. You just missed out on a chance to meet a cool kid, Vernon."

"Not my problem." Vern chuckled. "But if you want to meet up sometime, Killian, I'd definitely be interested."

"Ugh." Kylie tapped the screen to end the call and met Erick's gaze. "I'm sorry you had to hear that."

Tom pulled her close and wrapped an arm around her shoulders. "It's probably better for everyone to know what kind of person Tallbaum is. You did great."

Erick nodded. "Thanks. It was pretty cool of you to do something you didn't want just because it was what I wanted. I'm sorry I made you do it. I guess I just didn't think someone could be as bad as you were acting like he was."

"You're old enough to make your own decisions about what you want from me."

"Thanks." Erick brought a finger to his mouth to chew on a hangnail. "So, I was wondering how far you're willing to go."

"About what?"

"I need a place to live. I'm getting tired of the foster home I'm in. I don't have any privacy."

Kylie grinned and barely stopped herself from clapping her hands. "I have a spare bedroom."

Tom offered his hand to Erick. "If you want to be part of our family, I'm willing to figure out how to make it work."

Erick gazed at Tom's outstretched hand with narrowed eyes. "But what if it doesn't work out? What if you decide you were better off without me?"

Kylie crossed over to him and pulled him into her arms. Erick froze, and Kylie held her breath but didn't back away from him. She needed to hug him, and he needed to know she loved him, even if it was scary. "It will work out, and I'll never think I was better off without you. I have always loved you, Erick. If you move in with us, I'm going to get my parental rights back. I'm going to be your mother forever, but you get to make the choice of whether or not you want to move in with me."

Tom nodded. "If you move in with *us*, we're going to be a family. So you're going to want to think things over carefully before you make a decision."

Kylie held her breath as Erick shifted in her arms. She didn't want to let him go, but instead of moving away from her, he brought his arms up, wrapped them around her back, and pressed his head against her chest.

Barely able to swallow her sobs, Kylie bent her head to kiss the top of his. "I can't promise that it'll be easy, but I promise we'll make it work."

Tom wrapped an arm around each of them, and the three of them stood together in the conference room for quite a while. For the first time since she'd learned she was pregnant, Kylie honestly believed everything would be okay.

Epilogue

KYLIE CARRIED A pitcher of lemonade out to set on the picnic table. It was Labor Day weekend, and they were hosting a party to celebrate their wedding.

It hadn't been the traditional wedding Kylie had always dreamed of, but she was happy with it. First thing that morning, the three of them had finalized Tom's adoption of Erick at the courthouse in Duluth, then the two of them had been married in a judge's chambers.

No frilly white dress or cotillion of wedding attendants could make her love Tom any more than him vowing to love and honor Erick as his own son forever.

Erick and a group of his friends were down at the lake, swimming. Tom, Erick, and Kylie had been living together for six and a half months. The first few months were tough as they adjusted to each other, but the summer had been pretty relaxed and enjoyable for all of them.

Tom was running Mallock Manufacturing again. Lance seemed to have forgiven the two of them for getting back together, but the brothers didn't spend much time together anymore. Hazel and Gil Mallock were on the deck with Tom's sisters and their families. Keefe and Mira were chatting with Kylie's parents over by the garage.

Kylie stood there, looking around, stunned by the number of people who'd shown up. Tom walked up behind her and wrapped his arms around her waist. "What a great day, Mrs. Mallock," he said before brushing her hair out of the way to kiss her neck.

"Yeah." She'd never expected her family to show up or for Tom to reconcile with his parents, yet there they all were.

She smiled sadly, wishing Scott and Kristy were there too, but it wasn't meant to be. Scott was in jail for assaulting Vern.

"Hey, look." Tom turned Kylie toward the driveway, where Scott was getting out of his car.

"What's he doing here?" she asked.

"Didn't you invite him?"

"No. I thought he was still in jail."

"Go talk to him."

Kylie took a deep breath and stepped away from Tom. She shivered even though the sun was high. Scott glanced around and moved toward Keefe and Mira but stopped as Kylie walked down the sidewalk toward him. He nodded at Keefe then turned to walk to Kylie. When they met in the middle of the sidewalk, he said, "The place looks great."

"Thanks. This is the best it's looked in a long time."

"Like I remember it as a kid. Everyone running around, having a great time." He looked down toward the lake.

"I missed that part of it."

"Me too," he admitted.

"Do you want a beer or something? There are coolers on the deck."

"Sure."

She turned to lead him to the coolers, and he grabbed her hand. When she faced him again, he pulled her into a hug. "I missed you."

She tried unsuccessfully to fight back her tears. "I missed you too."

"It's okay. We can make up for it now."

"Where's Sunny?"

Scott frowned. "She didn't want to stick around and wait for me. Last I heard, she'd headed to Wyoming."

"That sucks."

He shrugged. "It is what it is. Are you guys staying here?"

"Yeah. It's a nice place to raise kids. Erick's doing well."

Erick ran by with a couple of his friends.

"Which one is your son?"

"The tall one with red hair. He reminds me of you." She didn't say how worried she'd been that every time she had looked at Erick after he'd come to live with her, she'd see Vern looming over her. But now, all she saw was Erick. He was his own person and didn't remind her of his biological father at all. Instead, he reminded her of Scott at his age. Erick had picked up on some of Tom's mannerisms, and the two of them were fly-fishing fanatics.

"Well, let's hope he has a better understanding of family than I did."

Kylie squeezed her younger brother's hand as Tom joined them. "You'll just have to stick around and help teach him that it's never too late to have a family."

~The End~

Thank you for taking the time to read this book. A review would be greatly appreciated.

Want to read more by Lana?

The following books are currently available.

Alaskan Healing (An Alaskan Healing Novel)

Alaskan Hope (An Alaskan Healing Novel)

Alaskan Waves (An Alaskan Healing Novel)

Alaskan Recovery (An Alaskan Healing Novel)

Faceoff of the Heart

Letting Go

Away from Here

Want to know when Lana releases another book?

Sign up for her newsletter at her website www.lanavoynich.com.

Made in the USA
Charleston, SC
08 January 2017